FAIRY TALES OF
EASTERN EUROPE

FAIRY TALES OF
EASTERN EUROPE

Selected and retold by
Neil Philip
Illustrated by Larry Wilkes

CLARION BOOKS
NEW YORK

For William and Thomas
N.P.

For family and friends in Poland and
Czechoslovakia
L.W.

Clarion Books
a Houghton Mifflin Company imprint
215 Park Avenue South, New York, NY 10003

An Albion Book

Library of Congress Cataloging-in-Publication Data

Philip, Neil.
Fairy tales of Eastern Europe / selected and retold by Neil
Philip; illustrated by Larry Wilkes.
p.   cm.
Summary: A collection of fairy tales from Eastern Europe and the
Soviet Union, including "God's Cockerel" and
"Cinder Jack."
ISBN 0-395-57456-0
1. Fairy tales—Europe, Eastern. 2. Fairy tales—Soviet Union.
[1. Fairy tales. 2. Folklore—Europe, Eastern. 3. Folklore—Soviet
Union.] I. Wilkes, Larry, ill. II. Title.
PZ8.P54Fai   1991
398.21′0947—dc20
90-2664
CIP
AC
10 9 8 7 6 5 4 3 2 1

Typesetting and color origination by York House, London
Printed and bound in Hong Kong by South China Printing Co.

Contents

Introduction

"There was once, I don't know where, beyond seven times seven countries, and at a cock's crow even beyond them, an immense, tall, quivering poplar tree. This tree had seven times seventy-seven branches; on each branch there were seven times seventy-seven crows' nests, and in each nest seven times seventy-seven young crows. May those who don't listen attentively to my tale, or who doze, have their eyes pecked out by all those young crows; and those who listen with attention to my tale will never behold the land of the Lord!"

So might a Hungarian storyteller have begun his or her tale, to an audience of adults as well as children, at any time over hundreds of years.

The great poet Alexander Pushkin said of the Russian fairy tales, "Each one is a poem." The same is true of folktales wherever they are told. Though they may seem simple, even clumsy, compared to written stories, fairy stories are aptly called "wonder tales." They are full of the wonder of the world, and of existence, and of the transforming power of the human imagination. Through such stories, told in what the nineteenth century folklorist Joseph Jacobs called "bright trains of images," illiterate and uneducated men, women, and children have been able to explore what it means to be alive. The stories passed from mouth to mouth, and each time they were told they became something new, in a way that was both timeless and charged with the meaning of the passing moment.

This book is a collection of stories told in the countries of Eastern Europe and in the European part of what is now the Union of Soviet Socialist Republics. Most were recorded in the nineteenth century, as part of the great wave of folktale collecting which followed the publication of the Grimms' *Household Tales*. It is impossible in such a small sampling from such a wide area to do more than indicate the shadings of national and ethnic tradition, never mind the creative

11

voice of the individual storyteller. I hope, nevertheless, that these stories, which contain so much wisdom and experience in such an economical and beautiful form, will help paint an historical backdrop to the drama of today's news bulletins.

The heart of the book is the Slavic folk tradition, which roughly speaking breaks into three parts, along the lines of linguistic division. There are the Eastern Slavs of Russia, the Ukraine, and Byelorussia; the Southern Slavs of Bulgaria and what is now Yugoslavia; and the Western Slavs of Poland and Czechoslovakia. Each of these traditions has influenced and been influenced by its neighbors. The Bulgarians, for instance, poised between Russia and Greece, have absorbed traits from both. So I have not tried to make any firm division among them, and have even included two stories from Latvia and Lithuania, although these states, together with Estonia, should really be grouped with Finland. As Stith Thompson has noted in his great study, *The Folktale,* "In the small countries on the south shore of the Baltic, Russians and Germans and Poles have been continual borrowers and lenders of folktales." So my Lithuanian tale, "A Good Deed Is Always Requited with Ill," closely echoes a story in the classic Russian collection of Afanas'ev.

The tone of that story, with its use of fantasy, humor, and deadpan cynicism to explore a question of justice and morality, does seem to capture some of the essential flavor of the folklore of Eastern Europe. Here, stories which in other cultures are simply magical adventures are vehicles in which Fate, or Misery, or Need is personified, and takes a hand in human affairs. In one Slovak story in this book, the Twelve Months are actors in the old tale of the cruelly treated stepdaughter and her haughty, spoiled sister. In a Czech tale, Intelligence and Luck battle it out for supremacy; in a related Russian story, it is Luck and Bliss.

In one of Afanas'ev's short tales, the Sun, Wind, and Frost contest who is most powerful: the victor is the wind, which can temper both heat and cold. The Frost is a particularly powerful personification in such a cold climate, as Afanas'ev's famous story of "The Snow Maiden" or "Jack Frost" shows. W.R.S. Ralston writes in his *Russian Folk-Tales* how on Christmas Eve the oldest man in the house would take a spoonful of kissel (a sort of pudding) and lean out of the window with it, crying, "Frost, Frost, come and eat kissel! Frost, Frost, do not kill our oats! Drive our flax and hemp deep into the ground."

There is an earthiness, a sense of the realities of peasant life, running through these tales. Though there is magic in them, they do not, like the Irish fairy tales, leave reality behind in extravagant flights of imagination. When the hero of one of Afanas'ev's stories reaches Paradise, it is described in terms of the storyteller's everyday longing: "And what a tidy room it is! It's large and clean. The bed is wide and the pillows are of down." When in this book's story "The Cottage in the Sky" a peasant woman climbs a beanstalk to an upper world, she finds not treasure but a cottage made of food.

The twenty-two stories in this book do not even scrape the surface of the material that has been collected. Afanas'ev's collection, published between 1855 and 1866, alone contained some 640 tales, and an enormous amount of work has been carried out since. In Hungary, for instance, Sándor Erdész published 254 long narratives recorded from Lajos Ámi, an illiterate nightwatchman who was created a "Master of Folk Arts" by the cabinet of the Hungarian People's Republic in 1959. Likewise Linda Dégh published a whole volume of stories told by Mrs. Zsuzsanna Palkó in the Szekler settlement of Kakasd in Tolna County, and then examined and explored them in her important book, *Folktales and Society*.

In Russia, the entire repertoires of master storytellers such as M.M. Korguyev from Karelia and I.F. Kovolev from Gorky province have been collected and published, together with the narratives of two great women storytellers, Kupryanikha and Vinokurova. All of these storytellers, like their predecessors – including those anonymous men and women whose narratives have found their way into this book – brought their own creative skills to the task of entertaining their audience. Korguyev, for instance, modernized his tales both in tone, by concentrating on the psychology and motives of the folktale hero, and in detail. A.N. Nechayev, who published Korguyev's tales, writes that in one story, "He replaces the wooden eagle, upon which the hero of the tale usually does his journeying, by a two-seated airplane, with levers for steering 'to the right' and 'to the left.' "

Another less welcome change can be seen in some stories collected in this century, in which the independent art of the storyteller has been bullied into subservience to a political creed. Thus Y.M. Sokolov records in his *Russian Folklore* that in 1937 the well-known Russian narrator F.A. Konashkov told a long story on the folk theme of the quest in search of truth, "The Most Precious

14

Thing," in which the climax is the discovery that "the best and most precious thing we have on earth is the word of comrade Stalin."

One of the best and most precious things we do have on earth is the treasure trove of stories taken down by folklorists from the lips of narrators whose artistry would never otherwise have been known outside their own family and circle of friends. We do not know the name of any one of the tellers of my twenty-two stories, but we can be grateful to them all the same, and imagine each of them sitting down to tell us a tale, and finishing with a smile when "This is all the story; well, there are no more lies to tell."

NEIL PHILIP
Princes Risborough, 1991

The Origin of Man

Serbia

In the beginning there was nothing but God, and God slept and
dreamed. For ages and ages did this dream last. But it was fated that
He should wake up. Having roused Himself from sleep, He looked
about Him, and every glance became a star. God was amazed, and
began to travel, to see with His own eyes what He had created. He
traveled and traveled, but nowhere was there either end or limit. As
He traveled, He arrived at our earth. He was weary; sweat clung to
His brow. On the earth fell a drop of sweat. The drop became alive;
and this was the first man. He is God's kin, but he was not created
for pleasure. From the very beginning he was fated to toil and
sweat.

God's Cockerel

Serbia

The earth was waste; there was nothing but stone. God was sorry for this, and sent His cockerel to make the earth fruitful, as he knew how to do.

The cockerel came down into a cave in the rock, and fetched out an egg of wondrous power and purpose. The egg cracked, and seven rivers flowed out of it. The rivers watered the land, and soon all was green. There were all manner of flowers and fruits; the land, without man's labor, produced wheat, and on the trees grew not only apples and figs, but also the whitest and sweetest bread.

In this paradise men lived without care, working not from need but for amusement and merriment. Round the paradise were lofty mountains, so that there was no fear of violence or storm. And further, so that men, who were otherwise free and their own masters, might come to no harm, God's cockerel hovered high in the sky and crowed to them every day: when to get up, when to take their meals, what to do, and when to do it.

The nation was happy, except that God's cockerel annoyed them by his continual crowing. Men began to murmur, and pray God to deliver them from the restless creature. "Let us settle for ourselves," they said, "when to eat, to work, and to rise." God hearkened to them. The cock descended from the sky, but crowed to them just once more, "Woe is me! Beware of the lake!"

Men rejoiced, and said that the paradise was better than ever. Now, no one interfered with their freedom. Still, as of old, they ate, worked, and rose in good order, as the cock had taught them. But little by little, some of them began to think that it was unsuitable for a free people to obey the cock's crowing so slavishly, and began to live how they liked, observing no proper order.

Through this arose illnesses, and all kinds of distress; men looked again longingly to the sky, but God's cockerel was gone forever.

They wished, at least, to take heed of his last words, but they could not understand what they meant. The cock had warned them to beware of the lake, but why? There was no lake in the valley, only the seven rivers that had burst from the egg, each flowing quietly in its own channel. Men therefore thought there must be a dangerous lake somewhere on the other side of the mountains, and sent a man every day to the top of the hill to see what he could see. But there was no danger from any quarter; the man went in vain, and people calmed themselves again.

The people's pride grew greater and greater. The women made brooms from the wheat ears, and the men made straw mattresses. They no longer gathered bread from the tree in the old way, but instead set it on fire from below, so that the bread would fall and they might collect it without trouble. When they had eaten their fill, they lay down by the rivers and spoke all manner of foolish things.

One, looking at the river, wagged his head and jabbered, "Eh! Brothers! Isn't it a marvel! But what I'd like to know is, why is the flow of water always the same, neither more nor less?"

"That's just another craze of the cockerel's," answered one man. "It's shameful enough for us to live in fear of a lake that never was and never will be; if you listen to me, today will be the last time we send a watcher up the mountain. As regards the rivers, I think it would be better if there were more water."

The man next to him agreed at first, but then thought that as there was enough water already, more would be too much.

A fat man said excitedly that both were right. "The most sensible thing would be to break the egg up, and send just as much water as is wanted into each man's land. And there's certainly no need to send a watcher to look out for the lake any more."

When he stopped speaking, everyone cheered. They all rushed to the egg to break it to pieces, and the only thing they regretted was that it was too late to stop the watcher from going up the mountain that day.

The people stood around the egg, and the fat man took up a stone and banged it against the shell. It smashed with a crack of thunder, and so much water burst out of it that almost the whole human race perished. The paradise was filled with water and became one great lake. God's cockerel had warned truly, but in vain.

Soon the flood reached the highest mountains, just to the place where the watchman was standing, the only survivor from the destruction of mankind. Seeing the increasing waters, he fled.

Why Does a Cat Sit on the Doorstep in the Sun?

Romania

When Noah had built the ark, he kept the door wide open for the animals to enter. After they had all gone in, his own family came, and last of all his wife.

Noah said to her, "Come in." She obstinately said, "No." Noah again said, "Come in." She again said, "No." Noah, getting angry, said, "Oh, you devil, come in."

That was just what the devil was waiting for. He knew that Noah would not let him in otherwise, so he had waited for an invitation. He changed himself into a mouse, and followed Noah's wife into the ark.

When the devil has nothing to do, he weighs his tail. But here he found plenty to do. He thought, now is my chance to put an end to all of God's creatures. So he started gnawing on one of the planks, trying to make a hole in it.

When Noah surprised him at this devilish work, he threw his fur glove at the mouse. The glove turned into a cat, and in the twinkling of an eye, the mouse was in the cat's mouth.

But Noah would not allow the peace of the ark to be broken; the animals had to live in peace with one another. So he seized the cat, with the mouse in her mouth, and flung her out of the ark into the water.

The cat let go of the mouse, swam back to the ark, climbed onto the doorstep, and lay down to dry herself in the sun.

There she remained until the water had subsided, and ever since then, the cat likes to lie on the doorstep of the house and bask in the sun.

The Twelve Months

Czechoslovakia

Once upon a time there lived a mother who had two daughters. One was her own child, the other her stepdaughter. She was very fond of her own daughter, but she would not so much as look at her stepdaughter. The only reason was that Marusa, the stepdaughter, was prettier than her own daughter, Holena.

The gentle-hearted Marusa did not know how beautiful she was, and so she could never make out why her mother was so cross with her whenever she looked at her. She had to do all the housework, tidying up the cottage, cooking, washing, and sewing, and then she had to take the hay to the cow and look after her. She did all this work alone, while Holena spent the time adorning herself and lazing about. But Marusa liked work, for she was a patient girl, and when her mother scolded her she bore it like a lamb. It was no good, however, for her mother's taunts grew crueler and crueler every day, only because Marusa was growing prettier and Holena uglier every day.

At last the mother thought, "Why should I keep a pretty stepdaughter in my house? When the lads come courting here, they will fall in love with Marusa and they won't look at Holena."

From that moment the stepmother and her daughter were constantly scheming how to get rid of poor Marusa. They starved her and they beat her. But she bore it all, and in spite of all she kept on growing prettier every day. They invented torments that the cruelest of men would never have thought of.

One day – it was in the middle of January – Holena felt a longing for the scent of violets.

"Go, Marusa, and get me some violets from the forest; I want to wear them at my waist and to smell them," she said to her sister.

"Great heavens, sister! What a strange notion! Who ever heard of violets growing under the snow?" said poor Marusa.

24

"You wretched tatterdemalion! How dare you argue when I tell you to do something? Off you go at once, and if you don't bring me violets from the forest I'll kill you!" threatened Holena.

The stepmother caught hold of Marusa, turned her out of the door, and slammed it shut behind her. Marusa went into the forest, weeping bitterly. The snow lay deep, and there wasn't a human footprint to be seen. She wandered about for a long time, tortured by hunger and trembling with cold. She begged God to take her from the world.

At last she saw a light in the distance. She went towards the glow, and came to the top of a mountain. A big fire was burning there, and around the fire were twelve stones with twelve men sitting on them. Three of them had snow-white beards, three were not so old, and three were still younger. The three youngest were the handsomest of all. They were not speaking, but all sitting silent. These twelve men were the twelve months. Great January sat highest of all; his hair and beard were as white as snow, and in his hand he held a club.

Marusa was frightened. She stood still for a time in terror, but, growing bolder, she went up to them and said, "Please, kind sirs, let me warm my hands at your fire. I am trembling with the cold."

Great January nodded, and asked her, "Why have you come here, my dear little girl? What are you looking for?"

"I am looking for violets," answered Marusa.

"This is no time to be looking for violets, for everything is covered with snow," answered Great January.

"Yes, I know; but my sister Holena and my stepmother said that I must bring them some violets from the forest. If I don't bring them, they'll kill me. Tell me, fathers, please tell me where I can find them."

Great January stood up and went to one of the younger months – it was March – and, giving him the club, he said, "Brother, take the high seat."

March took the high seat upon the stone and waved the club over the fire. The fire blazed up, the snow began to melt, the trees began to bud, the ground under the young beech trees was at once covered with grass, and the crimson daisy buds began to peep through the grass. It was springtime. Under the bushes the violets were blooming among their little leaves, and before Marusa had time to think, so many of them had sprung up that they looked like a blue cloth spread out on the ground.

"Pick them quickly, Marusa!" commanded March.

Marusa picked them joyfully till she had a big bunch. Then she thanked the months with all her heart and scampered merrily home.

Holena and the stepmother wondered when they saw Marusa bringing the violets. They opened the door to her, and the scent of violets filled all the cottage.

"Where did you get them?" asked Holena sulkily.

"They are growing under the bushes in a forest on the high mountains."

Holena put them in her waistband. She let her mother smell them, but she did not say to her sister, "Smell them."

The next day she was lolling near the stove, and now she longed for some strawberries. So she called to her sister and said, "Go, Marusa, and get me some strawberries from the forest."

"Alas! Dear sister, where could I find any strawberries? Who ever heard of strawberries growing under the snow?" said Marusa.

"You wretched little tatterdemalion, how dare you argue when I tell you to do a thing? Go at once and get me the strawberries, or I'll kill you!"

The stepmother caught hold of Marusa and pushed her out of the

door and shut it after her. Marusa went to the forest, weeping bitterly. The snow was lying deep, and there wasn't a human footprint to be seen anywhere. She wandered about for a long time, tortured by hunger and trembling with cold. At last she saw the light she had seen the day before. Overjoyed, she went toward it. She came to the great fire with the twelve months sitting around it.

"Please, kind sirs, let me warm my hands at the fire. I am trembling with cold."

Great January nodded, and asked her, "Why have you come again, and what are you looking for here?"

"I am looking for strawberries."

"But it is winter now, and strawberries don't grow in the snow," said January.

"Yes, I know," said Marusa sadly, "but my sister Holena and my stepmother bade me bring them some strawberries, and if I don't bring them, they will kill me. Tell me, fathers, tell me, please, where I can find them."

Great January arose. He went over to the month sitting opposite him – it was June – and handed the club to him, saying, "Brother, take the high seat."

June took the high seat upon the stone and swung the club over the fire. The fire shot up, and its heat melted the snow in a moment. The ground was all green, the trees were covered with leaves, the birds began to sing, and the forest was filled with all kinds of flowers. It was summer. The ground under the bushes was starred with white, the starry blossoms were turning into strawberries every minute. They ripened at once, and before Marusa had time to think, there were so many of them that it looked as though blood had been sprinkled on the ground.

"Pick them at once, Marusa!" commanded June.

Marusa picked them joyfully till she had filled her apron. Then she thanked the months with all her heart and scampered merrily home.

Holena and the stepmother wondered when they saw Marusa bringing the strawberries. Her apron was full of them. They ran to open the door for her, and the scent of the strawberries filled the whole cottage.

"Where did you pick them?" asked Holena sulkily.

"There are plenty of them growing under the young beech trees in the forest on the high mountains."

Holena took the strawberries and went on eating them till she could eat no more. So did the stepmother, but they didn't say to Marusa, "Here is one for you."

When Holena had enjoyed the strawberries, she grew greedy for other dainties, and so on the third day she longed for some red apples.

"Marusa, go into the forest and get me some red apples," she said to her sister.

"Alas! Sister dear, how am I to get apples for you in winter?" protested Marusa.

"You wretched little tatterdemalion, how dare you argue when I tell you to do a thing? Go to the forest at once, and if you don't bring me the apples I will kill you!" threatened Holena.

The stepmother caught hold of Marusa and pushed her out of the door and shut it after her. Marusa went to the forest, weeping bitterly. The snow was lying deep; there wasn't a human footprint to be seen anywhere. But she didn't wander about this time. She ran straight to the top of the mountain where the big fire was burning. The twelve months were sitting around the fire; yes, there they certainly were, and Great January was sitting on the high seat.

"Please, kind sirs, let me warm my hands at the fire. I am trembling with cold."

Great January nodded, and asked her, "Why have you come here, and what are you looking for?"

"I am looking for red apples."

"It is winter now, and red apples don't grow in winter," answered January.

"Yes, I know," said Marusa sadly, "but my sister and my stepmother bade me bring them some red apples from the forest. If I don't bring them, they will kill me. Tell me, fathers, tell me, please, where I could find them."

Great January rose up. He went over to one of the older months – it was September. He handed the club to him and said, "Brother, take the high seat."

September took the high seat upon the stone and swung the club over the fire. The fire began to burn with a red flame; the snow

29

began to melt. But the trees were not covered with leaves; the leaves were wavering down one after the other, and the cold wind was driving them to and fro over the yellowing ground. This time Marusa did not see so many flowers. Only red pinks were blooming on the hillside, and meadow saffrons were flowering in the valley. High fern and thick ivy were growing under the young beech trees. But Marusa was only looking for red apples, and at last she saw an apple tree with red apples hanging high among its branches.

"Shake the tree at once, Marusa!" commanded September.

Right gladly Marusa shook the tree, and one apple fell down.

She shook it a second time, and another apple fell down.

"Now, Marusa, run home quickly!" shouted the month.

Marusa obeyed at once. She picked up the apples, thanked the months with all her heart, and ran merrily home.

Holena and the stepmother wondered when they saw Marusa bringing the apples. They ran to open the door for her, and she gave them the two apples.

"Where did you get them?" asked Holena.

"There are plenty of them in the forest on the high mountain."

"And why didn't you bring more? Or did you eat them on the way home?" said Holena harshly.

"Alas! Sister dear, I didn't eat a single one. But when I had shaken the tree once, one apple fell down, and when I shook it a second time, another apple fell down, and they wouldn't let me shake it again. They shouted to me to go straight home," protested Marusa.

Holena began to curse her. "May you be struck to death by lightning!" she shouted, and she was going to beat her.

Marusa began to cry bitterly, and she prayed to God to take her to Himself, or she would be killed by her wicked sister and her stepmother. She ran away into the kitchen.

Greedy Holena stopped cursing and began to eat the apple. It tasted so delicious that she told her mother she had never tasted anything so nice in all her life. The stepmother liked her apple too. When they had finished, they wanted some more.

"Mother, give me my fur coat. I'll go to the forest myself. That ragged little wretch would eat them all up again on her way home. I'll find the place all right, and I'll shake them all down, however they shout at me."

Her mother tried to dissuade her, but it was no good. She took her fur coat, wrapped a cloth round her head, and off she went to the forest. Her mother stood on the threshold, watching to see how Holena would manage to walk in the wintry weather.

The snow lay deep, and there wasn't a human footprint to be seen anywhere. Holena wandered about for a long time, but her desire for the sweet apples kept driving her on. At last she saw a light in the distance. She went toward it, and climbed to the top of the mountain where the big fire was burning, and around the fire on twelve stones the twelve months were sitting. She was terrified at

31

first, but she soon recovered. She stepped up to the fire and stretched out her hands to warm them, but she didn't say as much as "By your leave" to the twelve months; no, she didn't say a single word to them.

"Why have you come here, and what are you looking for?" asked Great January crossly.

"Why do you want to know, you old fool? It's no business of yours," replied Holena angrily, and she turned away from the fire and went into the forest.

Great January frowned and swung the club over his head. The sky grew dark in a moment, the fire burned low, the snow began to fall as thick as if the feathers had been shaken out of a down quilt, and an icy wind began to blow through the forest. Holena couldn't see one step in front of her; she lost her way altogether, and several times she fell into snowdrifts. Then her limbs grew weak and began slowly to stiffen. The snow kept on falling and the icy wind blew more icily than ever. Holena began to curse Marusa and the Lord God. Her limbs began to freeze, despite her fur coat.

Holena's mother was waiting for her; she kept on looking out for her, first at the window, then outside the door, but all in vain.

"Does she like the apples so much that she can't leave them, or what is the matter? I must see for myself where she is," decided the stepmother at last. So she put on her fur coat, wrapped a shawl round her head, and went out to look for Holena. The snow was lying deep; there wasn't a human footprint to be seen; the snow fell fast, and the icy wind was blowing through the forest.

Marusa had cooked the dinner, she had seen to the cow, and yet Holena and her mother did not come back. "Where are they staying so long?" thought Marusa, as she sat down to work at the distaff. The spindle was full already and it was quite dark in the room, and yet Holena and the stepmother had not come back.

"Alas, Lord! What has happened to them?" cried Marusa, peering anxiously through the window. The sky was bright and the earth was all glittering, but there wasn't a human soul to be seen. Sadly she shut the window; she crossed herself and prayed for her sister and her mother. In the morning she waited with breakfast, she waited with dinner; but however long she waited, it was no good. Neither her mother nor her sister ever came back. Both of them were frozen to death in the forest.

So good Marusa inherited the cottage, a piece of plowland, and the cow. She married a kind husband, and they both lived happily ever after.

Intelligence and Luck

Czechoslovakia

Once upon a time Luck met Intelligence on a garden seat. "Move over!" said Luck. Intelligence was still wet behind the ears, and didn't know who was boss.

"Why should I make room for you? You're no better than me," he said.

"We'll see about that," answered Luck. "The proof of the pudding is in the eating. Look at the peasant's son plowing in that field. You go with him, and if he gets on better with you than he would with me, I'll always make way for you, whenever and wherever we meet."

Intelligence agreed, and entered at once into the plowboy's head. As soon as the plowboy felt that he had intelligence in his head, he began to think, "Why must I follow the plow till the day I die? I can go somewhere else and make my fortune more easily."

He stopped plowing, put up the plow, and went home. "Daddy," he said, "I don't like this peasant's life; I'd rather learn to be a gardener."

His father said, "What is up with you, Vanek? Have you gone mad?" However, he thought it over, and said, "Well, if it's what you want, learn, and God be with you! Your brother will inherit the cottage after me."

Vanek lost the cottage, but he didn't care about that. He bound himself apprentice to the king's gardener. For every little thing that the gardener showed him, Vanek understood ever so much more. Before long he didn't even obey the gardener's orders, but did everything his own way. At first the gardener was angry, but, seeing the garden getting on so much better, he was content. "I see that you have more intelligence than I," he said, and after that he let Vanek garden as he thought fit.

Before long, Vanek had made the garden so beautiful that the

king took great delight in it, and frequently walked in it with the queen and their only daughter.

The princess was a very beautiful girl, but since the age of twelve she had been mute, and no one ever heard a single word from her. The king was very sad, and had it proclaimed that whoever could get her to speak again should be her husband. Many young kings, princes, and other great lords tried one after the other, but all went away as they had come; no one succeeded in making her speak.

"Why shouldn't I too try my luck?" thought Vanek. "You never know, I may be able to get her to answer a question." He went straight to the palace, and the king and his councillors took him to the room where the princess was.

The king's daughter had a pretty little dog, which she was very fond of, because he was so clever and understood everything that she wanted. When Vanek went into the room with the king and his councillors, he acted as though he didn't even see the princess, but turned to the dog and said, "I have heard, doggie, that you are very clever, and I have come to you for advice.

"We were three traveling companions, a sculptor, a tailor, and myself. Once upon a time we were going through a forest and were obliged to pass the night there. To be safe from wolves, we made a fire, and agreed to keep watch one after the other. The sculptor kept watch first, and to kill time took a log and carved a girl out of it. When it was finished he woke the tailor to keep watch in his turn. The tailor, seeing the wooden girl, asked what it was.

" 'As you see,' said the sculptor, 'I was weary, and didn't know what to do with myself, so I carved a girl out of a log; if you find time hanging heavy on your hands, you can dress her.' The tailor at once took out his scissors, needle, and thread, cut out the clothes; stitched away; and when they were ready, dressed the girl in them. He then called me to come and keep watch. I, too, asked him what the meaning of all this was.

" 'As you see,' said the tailor, 'the sculptor found time hanging heavy on his hands and carved a girl out of a log, and I for the same reason clothed her. If you find time dragging, you can teach her to speak.' And by dawn I had actually taught her to speak.

"Well, in the morning when my companions woke up, each wanted to keep the girl. The sculptor said, 'I made her.' The tailor said, 'I clothed her.' I, too, maintained my right to keep her.

"Tell me, therefore, doggie: to which of us does the girl belong?"

The dog said nothing, but the princess replied, "To whom can she belong but to yourself? What's the good of the tailor's dressing without speech? You gave her the best gift, life and speech, and therefore she by right belongs to you."

"You have passed your own sentence," said Vanek. "I have given you speech again and a new life, and you therefore by right belong to me."

Then one of the king's councillors said, "His Royal Grace will give you a rich reward for unloosing his daughter's tongue, but you cannot marry her, as you are only a peasant's son."

The king said the same. But Vanek wouldn't hear of any other reward. He said, "The king promised without any exception, that whoever made his daughter speak again should be her husband. A king's word is law; and if the king wants others to observe his laws, he must first keep them himself. Therefore the king must give me his daughter."

"Seize and bind him!" shouted the councillor. "Whoever says the king *must* do anything, offers an insult to His Majesty, and should die! May it please Your Majesty to order this malefactor to be executed with the sword?"

The king said, "Let him be executed."

Vanek was immediately bound and led away. When they came to the place of execution, Luck was there waiting for him, and said secretly to Intelligence, "See how this man has got on through you, till he has to lose his head! Make way, and let me take your place!"

As soon as Luck entered Vanek, the executioner's sword broke against the scaffold, just as if someone had snapped it. Before they could bring him another, up rode a trumpeter on horseback from the city, galloping as swift as a bird, trumpeting merrily, and waving a white flag; and after him came the royal carriage for Vanek.

This is what had happened. The princess had told her father at home that Vanek had but spoken the truth, and that the king's word ought not to be broken. If Vanek were a peasant's son, the king could easily make him a prince.

The king said, "You're right. Let him be a prince!"

The royal carriage was immediately sent for Vanek, and the councillor who had set the king against him was executed in his stead.

Afterward, when Vanek and the princess were leaving the wedding together in a carriage, Intelligence happened to be on the road, and seeing that he couldn't help meeting Luck, bent his head and slipped to one side, just as if cold water had been thrown upon him. And from that time forth it is said that Intelligence has always given way to Luck whenever he has had to meet him.

The Wishes

Hungary

There were ten thousand wagons rolling along the turnpike road. In each wagon there were ten thousand casks, in each cask ten thousand bags, in each bag ten thousand poppy seeds, and in each poppy seed ten thousand lightnings. May all those lightnings strike him who won't listen to my tale, which I have brought from beyond the Operencian sea!

There was once, and it doesn't matter where, but once upon a time, a poor man who had a pretty young wife; they were very fond of each other. The only thing they had to complain of was their poverty, as neither of them owned a thing. It happened, therefore, that sometimes they quarreled, and always when they quarreled they cast it in each other's teeth that they hadn't got anything to bless themselves with. But still they loved each other.

One evening, the woman came home much earlier than her husband, and went into the kitchen and lit the fire, even though there was no food to cook. "I can cook a little soup, at least, for my husband. It will be ready by the time he comes home," she thought. But no sooner had she put the kettle over the fire, and a few logs of wood on the fire to make the water boil quicker, than her husband arrived home and took his seat by her side on the little bench.

They warmed themselves by the fire, as it was late in the autumn, and cold; in the neighboring village they had started to harvest the grapes on that very day. "Do you know what has happened, wife?" asked the husband.

"No, I don't. I've heard nothing. Tell me what it is."

"As I was coming from the lord's maize field, I saw in the dark, in the distance, a black spot on the road. I couldn't make out what it was, so I went nearer, and lo! Do you know what it was? A beautiful little golden carriage, with a pretty little woman inside, and four fine black dogs harnessed to it."

38

"You're joking," said the wife.

"I'm not, it's perfectly true. You know how muddy the roads are about here; well, the dogs and the carriage were stuck fast in the mud and couldn't move, and the little woman didn't want to get out into the mud and soil her golden dress. At first when I saw them, I had a good mind to run away. I thought she might be an evil spirit. But she called out to me, and begged me to help her out of the mud. She promised that no harm would come to me, and that she would reward me. So I thought that it would be a good thing for us if she could help us in our poverty, and with my assistance the dogs dragged her carriage out of the mud. The woman asked me whether I was married. I told her I was. And she asked me whether I was rich. I replied, not at all; I didn't think, I said, that there were two people in the village who were poorer than we. 'That can be remedied,' said she. 'I will fulfill three wishes that your wife may propose.' And with that she left, as suddenly as if dragons had kidnapped her; I think she was a fairy."

"Well, she made a regular fool out of you."

"That remains to be seen. You must try to wish something, my dear wife."

Without giving it any thought, the woman said, "Well, I should like to have some sausage; we could cook it beautifully on this nice fire." No sooner were the words out of her mouth than a frying pan came down the chimney, with a sausage curled in it that was so long you could have used it to fence in the whole garden.

"This is grand!" they both exclaimed.

"But we must be a little more clever with our next two wishes," said the husband. "How rich we shall be! The first thing I will do is to buy two heifers and two horses, as well as a sucking pig." And with that he took his pipe from his hatband, took out his tobacco pouch, and filled his pipe. Then he tried to light it with a hot cinder, but he was so excited it made him clumsy, and he knocked over the frying pan with the sausage in it.

"Good heavens, the sausage! What on earth are you doing!" cried his wife in fright. "I wish that sausage would grow on your nose!" With that she tried to snatch the sausage from the fire, but it was too late. It was already dangling from her husband's nose down to his toes. "My Lord Creator help me!" shouted the woman.

"Look what you've done, you fool!" said her husband. "Now the second wish is gone. And what shall we do with this thing?"

"Can't we get it off?" said the woman.

"The devil we can!" raged her husband. "Don't you see it is growing from my nose; you can't take it off."

"Then we must cut it off," said she, "if we can do nothing else."

"I shan't permit it! How could I allow my body to be cut about? Not for all the treasures on earth," he replied. "But there is something we can do, love. There is one wish left. You must wish the sausage back in the pan, and then everything will be all right."

But the woman replied, "What about the heifers and the horses, and the sucking pig? How shall we get them?"

"Well, I can't walk about with this ornament. I'm sure you'll never kiss me again with this sausage dangling from my nose."

And so they quarreled for a long time, but at last the husband succeeded in persuading his wife to wish that the sausage was back in the pan. And so all three wishes were fulfilled, and yet they were as poor as ever.

But at least they made a good meal of the sausage, and afterward they thought that, as it was because they had quarreled that they had lost the heifers, and the horses, and the sucking pig, from now on they would quarrel no more. And because they worked hard, and saved hard, and didn't quarrel, in time they got on in the world, and owned two heifers, and two horses, and a sucking pig into the bargain.

The Flying Ship

Ukraine

Once there lived an old man and his wife, who had two sensible sons and a third son who was a fool. The woman loved her elder sons and kept their clothes clean, but she dressed the third son in cast-offs, and let him go about in a shirt which was black with dirt.

The family heard that a proclamation had been issued by the Tsar: "If anyone can build a ship capable of flying through the air, he shall receive as reward the hand of the Tsar's daughter."

The elder brothers decided to set out and try their luck in the construction of a flying ship. Their parents gave them their blessing, and afterwards furnished them with white rolls, and different kinds of meat, and a flask of spirits, and started them on their way.

Having seen all this, the fool begged that he too should be allowed to make the attempt. His mother tried to dissuade him. "How can a fool like you go?" she asked. "The wolves would eat you."

But the fool kept repeating the words, "I will go, yes, I will go!", and when his mother saw that she could not control him, she gave him a bottle of water and some black bread and showed him the door.

After he had gone a long way, the fool met an old man. They greeted each other, and the old man said, "Where are you going?"

"Well, you see, the Tsar has promised his daughter to the man who shall make a flying ship."

"But do you think you can make such a vessel?"

"No, I shall not be able to make one."

"Then why do you go?"

"God knows!"

"In that case," said the old man, "sit down here. Let us rest together and eat. Take out what is in your basket."

The fool answered, "I am ashamed to show you what I have."

"Never mind; take it out; let us eat what God has given."

The fool opened the basket, and could not believe his eyes: instead of coarse black bread he saw soft white rolls, and all sorts of good things. He handed some of the provisions to the old man. "You see," said the latter, "how God takes care of fools! Although your own mother does not love you, you are not forsaken. Let's have a strong drink." And lo and behold, the bottle contained spirits, though only water had been put in it. So the pair drank, and ate.

Then the old man said to the fool. "Listen! Enter the forest and, walking to the first tree, cross yourself three times and strike the tree with a hatchet; next, fall with your face to the ground and lie there until somebody wakes you. You will then see near you a flying ship, all ready for you. Take your seat and fly wherever you wish; and take on board everyone you meet on the way."

The fool thanked the old man, bade him farewell, and walked into the forest. He went up to the nearest tree and followed the old man's instructions. He crossed himself three times, tapped the tree with a hatchet, lay down with his face toward the ground, and went to sleep.

A little later, someone roused him. The fool woke, and saw a ship ready. Without delay, he entered and set off through the air.

He flew on and on, till he saw a man lying below him with his ear pressed to the raw ground. "Greetings, granddad!" said the fool.

"Greetings to you, in the sky!"

"What are you doing?" the fool called out.

"I am listening to everything that is taking place on the earth."

"Leave that, and come and sit with me in the flying ship!"

Accepting the invitation, the man embarked, and the ship flew on.

As they flew farther, the fool saw below him a man hopping on one foot, the other foot being fastened to his ear.

"Greetings, old man!" cried the fool. "Why are you hopping about on one foot?"

"Were I to unfasten the other foot, I should step across the whole world at a stride."

"Come and sit with me!"

The man took his place, and the ship continued its flight.

Before long, the fool saw below him a man who was aiming a gun, but what he was aiming at could not be seen. "Greetings, friend," shouted the fool. "What are you aiming at? There's not a single bird in sight."

"That would be too easy," replied the man. "But if I kill a bird or beast a thousand versts away, then I consider myself a good shot!"

"Come and sit with us," said the fool.

The man took his place, and the party flew on farther, till they saw a man carrying a bag of bread upon his back. "Greetings, friend. Where are you going?" called out the fool.

"I am going to get bread for dinner," came the answer.

"But you have a bag full of bread already on your back!"

"This is not enough to make a meal for me; this is just for the journey."

"Take a seat with us," said the fool, and the man with the large appetite took his place in the ship.

They flew on and on till they noticed a man walking round a lake. "Greetings, brother! What are you looking for?" called the fool.

"I am thirsty and cannot find any water."

"But there is a whole lake beside you. Why do you not drink?"

"The water in this lake would not make a mouthful for me."

"Then come and sit with us!"

The man climbed into the vessel, and it flew onward.

After a while the party noticed a man walking in the forest with a bundle of firewood on his shoulders. "Greetings, old man! Why are you carrying wood into the forest?"

"This is not ordinary wood."

"What kind is it, then?"

"If you throw this wood down, a whole army will suddenly appear."

"Come and take a seat," said the fool. The man entered, and the ship flew onward.

In time, the fool saw a man carrying a bag of straw, and shouted, "Greetings to you, master! Where are you taking that straw?"

"To a village."

"Why? Is there no straw there?"

"This is not ordinary straw. If you throw it about, at once the weather becomes cold, with snow and ice."

"Take a seat with us," cried the fool.

"Thank you!" This was the last meeting, and the party flew quickly to the Tsar's court.

The Tsar was at dinner. He saw the flying ship and, in astonishment, sent a servant to make enquiries about it. The servant approached, but, seeing that the passengers were all peasants, did not stop to ask questions. He returned and reported to the Tsar that there was not a single noble on the ship, only working people.

The Tsar did not think it would be right to give his daughter in marriage to a humble peasant, and turned over in his mind how he would get rid of such a poor son-in-law. He decided to set the young man a series of difficult tasks, and first of all told his servant to order the fool to provide some water of life and health for the dinner.

The ship's first passenger, the one who listened to everything that was happening on earth, heard the Tsar's words, and repeated them to the fool. "What on earth shall I do?" wailed the simpleton. "If I look for a whole year, or a whole century, I'll never find any water of life and health."

"Do not fear," said the man of speed. "I will put the matter right for you."

The servant arrived and communicated the Tsar's order.

"Say that I will bring it," replied the fool.

Immediately, the man of speed unhitched his foot from his ear and, running off, reached the water of life and health in the twinkling of an eye. He collected some, and then, thinking he would have plenty of time to return, sat down to rest near a mill and went to sleep.

The Tsar's dinner was nearly over, and nothing had come. All was confusion on the ship. The first passenger placed his ear to the ground and listened, and said, "He has gone to sleep beside the mill."

At this, the sharpshooter seized his weapon, shot at the mill, and so roused the man of speed from his slumber. He ran back in a minute with the water, and it was on the table before the Tsar rose, so his order had been fulfilled, and there was nothing for him to do but to set another task.

The Tsar sent his servant with this order to the fool, "As you are

so skillful, give another exhibition of your powers. Consume, with
your companions, twelve roast bullocks and two tons of bread at
one meal.''

The first passenger heard and announced the message to the fool,
who was alarmed, and said, ''I do not eat even one loaf at a meal.''

''Have no fear,'' said the man with the large appetite. ''It will be a
small meal to me.''

So when the servant arrived with the Tsar's command, the fool
said, ''Very well. Deliver the provisions and we will eat them.''

Twelve roast bullocks and two tons of baked bread were sent. The
greedy man ate them all up, and said, ''It wasn't very much; I wish
there had been more!''

The Tsar then sent an order to the fool that he and his
companions must drink forty barrels of wine, each barrel containing
forty buckets. The first passenger overheard, and, as before,
informed the fool. The fool said in fear, ''I could not drink a whole
bucket of wine.''

''Do not be afraid,'' said the thirsty man, ''I will drink for all; the
task will be small for me.'' When forty barrels full of wine had been
brought, the thirsty man drank the lot without pausing, and said,
''It wasn't very much; I could have drunk more.''

After this, the Tsar didn't know what to do. So he ordered the
simpleton to go to the steam bath and wash. The bath was made of
cast iron, and the Tsar ordered it to be heated up so hot that it would
cause the fool to suffocate. While they were making the bath red-
hot, the fool came in to bathe, but he was followed by the peasant
with the straw.

When they were shut up in the bathroom, the peasant threw the straw about, and made it so cold that the water froze in the iron bath, and the fool could scarcely wash. To keep warm, he climbed onto the stove and lay there all night.

When the door was opened in the morning, the fool was alive and well, lying on the stove and singing songs. A report was made to the Tsar, who was very upset at his failure to get rid of the simpleton. At last he decreed that the fool could marry his daughter, but only if he could raise a whole regiment of soldiers; otherwise, he would lose his life.

When the fool heard of this order, he trembled with fear, and said, "I am altogether lost! You have rescued me several times from disaster, comrades; but it is now clear that you can do nothing."

"Why say that?" called out the peasant with the bundle of firewood. "Have you forgotten me? Remember my power in such matters, and do not be afraid."

The servant approached and told the fool of the Tsar's decree. "If you wish to wed the princess, you must supply a regiment of soldiers by tomorrow."

"Very well, I will do it! Only if the Tsar should make any further excuse, I will attack his whole kingdom and take the princess by force."

The peasant with the firewood went out into a field that night and scattered the wood in various directions. Immediately there appeared an innumerable host of soldiers, horse, foot, and artillery.

In the morning, the Tsar looked out and saw them, and trembled in his turn. Without delay he sent out costly presents and garments to the fool, and invited him to the palace for a marriage celebration with the princess.

The fool put on his finery, and a magnificent air, and went to the palace. The Tsar gave him a rich marriage gift, and all of a sudden he didn't seem such a fool after all. In fact the Tsar and Tsaritsa took quite a liking to him, and luckily the princess did too.

The Feather of Bright
Finist the Falcon

Russia

There lived an old man with his old wife. They had three daughters. The youngest was lovelier than tongue can tell, and prettier than a picture. Once the old man was going to town to the fair, and he said, "My dear daughters, tell me what you want, and I will buy it for you at the fair."

The eldest said, "Father, buy me a new dress." The second said, "Father, buy me a new shawl." But the youngest said, "Bring me a red flower."

The old man laughed at his youngest daughter. "Oh, you ninny! What do you want with a red flower? That's no use! You should ask for clothes."

No matter what he said, he could not persuade her. "Bring me a red flower, nothing but that."

The old man went to the fair, and bought the eldest daughter a dress and the second daughter a shawl, but in the whole town he could not find a red flower. Only as he was coming home did he happen across a strange man with a red flower in his hand. "Sell me your flower," he said.

"It is not for sale. But if your youngest daughter will marry my son, Bright Finist the Falcon, I will give you the flower as a gift."

The father grew thoughtful. Not to take the flower would grieve his daughter, but to take it was to give her in marriage, God knows to whom! He thought and thought, but still he took the flower. "What's the harm?" he asked himself. "They will come with proposals by and by. If he is not the right man, why, we can refuse."

He went home, and gave the eldest daughter her dress and the second her shawl. To the youngest he gave the flower, saying, "I don't like this flower, daughter, really I don't like it." He whispered in her ear, "The flower was not for sale. I took it from a strange man, after promising to give you in marriage to his son, Bright Finist the Falcon."

"Don't worry, Father. He is good and kind. He flies as a bright falcon in the sky, but when he touches the damp earth he becomes a hero of heroes."

"But do you know him?"

"I know him, Father. Last Sunday he was at Mass, and looked at me all the time. I talked to him; he loves me, Father."

The old man shook his head, looked at his daughter very sharply, made the sign of the cross on her forehead, and said, "Go to your room, my dear daughter, it is time to sleep. The morning is wiser than the evening; we will talk this matter over tomorrow."

The daughter shut herself up in her room, put the red flower in water, opened the window, and looked into the blue distance. Coming from who knows where, Bright Finist the Falcon of Flowery Feathers wheeled before her, sprang in through the window, struck the floor, and became a young man. The girl was frightened, but when he spoke her heart warmed with joy. They talked till dawn, and who knows what they said, save that at dawn Bright Finist the Falcon kissed her and said, "Every night as soon as the bright little flower is placed on the window I will fly to you, my dear. Here is a feather from my wing. Should you wish for a dress, go out on the balcony, wave the feather to the right, and whatever you wish for will appear.'' He kissed her once more, turned into a bright falcon, and flew away beyond the dark forest.

The girl gazed after her fated one, closed the window, and lay down to sleep. From that time, every night, as soon as she placed the little red flower at the window, the good youth, Bright Finist the Falcon, flew to her.

Well, Sunday came. The elder sisters began to dress for Mass. ''But what are you going to wear? You don't have anything new,'' they said to the youngest one.

She answered, ''Never mind. I can pray just as well at home.''

The elder sisters went to church, and the youngest sat at the window in an old dress and looked at the people going to church. She bided her time, went out on the porch, waved her colored

feather to the right, and from who knows where there appeared before her a crystal carriage, thoroughbred horses, servants in gold, a beautiful dress, and many jewels. In an instant, the beautiful girl was dressed and on her way to church. When she arrived, the people gaped at her beauty. "This must be some Tsar's daughter," they said.

As soon as the service was over, she left the church, sat in her carriage, and was whirled back home. The people went out to look at her and to see where she went, but she was gone, and her track was cold.

As soon as she was home our beauty took off her fine clothes, waved her bright feather to the left, and in a moment she was sitting as before, watching the people go home from church.

The sisters too came home. "Well, sister," they said, "what a beauty was at church today! She was lovelier than tongue can tell, and prettier than a picture. She must be some Tsar's daughter, she was so splendid."

The second and third Sundays came, and the beautiful girl again mystified the people at church, her sisters, her father, and her mother. But the last time she undressed she forgot to take the diamond pin from her hair. The elder sisters came home from church and told her of the Tsar's daughter, and then they saw the diamonds blazing in her hair.

"Oh, sister, what is this?" they cried. "Why, the Tsar's daughter was wearing just such a pin today. Where did you get it?"

The girl was confused, and ran to her room. Her sisters whispered and guessed, but she said nothing, and kept her secret with a smile. So the elder sisters began to watch her and to listen at her door, and they overheard her talking one night with Bright Finist the Falcon, and saw at dawn with their own eyes how he sprang from the window and flew off beyond the dark forest.

The elder sisters were jealous. They decided to hide knives on the window of their sister's room, so that Bright Finist the Falcon would cut his colored wings. They did this straightaway; the younger sister knew nothing about it. She put her red flower on the window, lay down on the couch, and fell sound asleep. Bright Finist the Falcon flew to the window, and as he was springing in, cut his left foot; but the younger sister knew nothing about it, she was enjoying

such a sweet calm sleep. Bright Finist the Falcon rose furiously into the sky, and flew beyond the dark forest.

In the morning the girl awoke. She looked around her. It was daylight already, and the good youth was not there. She looked at the window, and on it were two sharp knives across each other, and red blood dripping from them to the flower. Long did she shed her bitter tears; many nights did she wait sleepless by her window. But she waved the bright feather in vain: Bright Finist the Falcon flew no longer, and sent not his servants.

At last she went to her father with tears in her eyes and begged his blessing. She had forged three pairs of iron shoes, three iron staves, three iron caps, and three iron Easter cakes. She put a pair of shoes on her feet and a cap on her head, took a staff in her hand, and set off towards the dark forest.

She trudged through the slumbering forest, over stumps, over logs. One pair of iron shoes were trodden out, one iron cap was worn off, one staff was rusting away, one cake was gnawed to bits, and still the beautiful girl walked on, walked all the time, and the forest grew darker and denser.

All at once she saw standing before her an iron hut on hen's legs, turning without ceasing.

"Hut, hut!" she said. "Stand with your back to the forest, your front to me."

The hut turned its front to her. She entered the hut, and in it was lying a Baba-Yaga, from corner to corner, her lips on the crossbeam, her nose in the loft.

"Tfu-tfu-tfu! In the old days you couldn't hear or smell Russia here; but now the stink of Russia is right up my nose. Where are you going, beautiful girl? Are you flying from work or seeking work?"

"Oh, dear Grandmother, I had Bright Finist the Falcon of Flowery Feathers, but my sisters harmed him. Now I am seeking him."

"Oh, my child, you have far to go. Thrice nine lands must yet be passed! Bright Finist the Falcon of Flowery Feathers lives in the fiftieth kingdom in the eightieth land, and is now betrothed to the daughter of a Tsar."

The Baba-Yaga nourished and fed the girl with what God had sent, and put her to bed. Next morning, when the light was dawning, she roused her, gave her a present for the road – a small golden hammer and ten little diamond nails – and said, "When you come to the blue sea, the bride of Bright Finist the Falcon will come out to the shore to walk. Take the golden hammer and drive the diamond nails. She will try to buy them from you. Take no payment, only ask to see Bright Finist the Falcon. Now go, with God, to my second sister."

Again the girl went through the dark forest, farther and farther; the forest was darker and deeper, the treetops wound up to the sky. Now the second pair of shoes was almost trodden out, the second cap worn away, the second iron staff broken, the iron cake worn away; before the girl was an iron hut on hen's legs, turning without ceasing.

"Hut, oh hut!" she said. "Stop with your back to the trees and your front to me, so that I may creep in and eat."

The hut turned its back to the trees and its front to the maiden. She entered. In the hut lay a Baba-Yaga, from corner to corner, her lips on the crossbeam, her nose in the loft.

"Tfu-tfu-tfu! In the old days you couldn't hear or smell Russia here, but now its stink is everywhere. Where are you going, pretty girl?"

"Grandmother dear, I am seeking Bright Finist the Falcon."

"Oh! He is going to marry; they are having the maiden's party tonight," said the Baba-Yaga.

She gave the girl food and drink, and put her to sleep. At daybreak next morning she roused her, gave her a golden plate with a diamond ball, and told her firmly, "When you come to the shore of the blue sea, roll the diamond ball on the golden plate. The bride of Bright Finist the Falcon of Flowery Feathers will try to buy the plate and ball. Take nothing for them, only ask to see Bright Finist the Falcon. Now go, with God, to my eldest sister."

Again the girl went through the dark forest, farther and farther; the forest grew darker and deeper. Now the third pair of shoes was almost trodden out, the third cap was wearing off, the third staff was breaking, and the last cake was gnawed away. On hen's legs stood an iron hut, turning without ceasing.

"Hut, oh hut!" she cried. "Stand with your back to the trees and your face to me. I must creep in and eat bread."

The hut turned. In the hut lay another Baba-Yaga, from corner to corner, her lips on the crossbeam, her nose in the loft.

"Tfu-tfu-tfu! In the old days you couldn't hear or smell Russia here; now its stink is everywhere. Where are you going, beautiful girl?"

"Grandmother dear, I am seeking Bright Finist the Falcon."

"Oh, fair maiden, he has married a Tsar's daughter! Here is my magic steed; sit on him and go, with God."

The girl sat on the steed and shot away. The forest grew thinner and thinner.

Behold, the blue sea was before her. Broad and far it spread, and there in the distance, like fire, burned the golden roofs of the lofty, white-walled chambers of the palace of Bright Finist the Falcon.

She sat then on the shifting sand of the shore and hammered the diamond nails with the golden hammer. At once the Tsar's

daughter came with her nurses and maidens and servingwomen to the shore. She stopped and wanted to buy the diamond nails and the golden hammer.

"Tsar's daughter, let me but look at Bright Finist the Falcon, and I will give them for nothing," said the girl.

"Bright Finist the Falcon is sleeping at present, and is not to be disturbed. But if you give me your beautiful hammer and nails, I will show him to you."

She took the hammer and nails, ran to the palace, and stuck a magic pin into the clothes of Bright Finist the Falcon, so that he should sleep soundly and not wake; then she ordered her servants to take the beautiful girl through the palace to her husband, and went for her walk.

Long did the girl struggle, long did she weep over her dear one; she could not wake him in any way.

When the Tsar's daughter was tired of walking, she came home, sent away the girl, and pulled out the pin.

Bright Finist the Falcon woke. "Oh, how long I have slept! Someone was here," he said, "weeping over me all the time, and talking to me, but I could not open my eyes, so heavy with sleep."

"You were dreaming," said the Tsar's daughter. "No one was here."

Next day the beautiful maiden sat again on the shore of the blue sea, rolling the diamond ball on the golden plate.

The Tsar's daughter went out to walk. She saw the ball and plate and said, "Sell them to me."

"Let me look at Bright Finist the Falcon, and I will give them for nothing."

The Tsar's daughter agreed, and again she pierced the clothes of Bright Finist the Falcon with a magic pin. Again the beautiful girl wept bitterly over her dear one, but could not rouse him.

The third day she sat on the shore of the blue sea, so sad and sorrowful, she was feeding her steed with glowing coals. The Tsar's daughter, seeing that the steed was eating fire, wanted to buy him.

"Let me look on Bright Finist the Falcon, and I'll give the steed for nothing."

The Tsar's daughter agreed, ran to the palace, and said to her husband, "Let me look at your head." She sat down to look at his head, and stuck the magic pin in his hair. Straightaway he was in a deep sleep. Then she sent her servants for the beautiful girl.

The girl came, and tried to wake her dear. She hugged him and kissed him, crying bitterly, bitterly. He woke not.

Then she began to look at his head, and out fell the magic pin.

Bright Finist the Falcon woke at once. He saw the beautiful girl and was glad. She told him everything just as it happened: how her wicked sisters envied her, how she had wandered, and how she had exchanged gifts with the Tsar's daughter. He loved her more than ever before, kissed her sweet lips, and summoned all the princes and nobles and people of every degree. Then he asked, "What is your judgment? With which wife should I spend my life: with her who sold me, or her who bought me?"

All the princes, nobles, and people of every degree declared in one voice that he should take the woman who had bought him; but the one who had sold him, he should hang her on the gate and shoot her. Bright Finist the Falcon of Flowery Feathers did this.

A Clever Lass

Czechoslovakia

Once upon a time there was a shepherd. He used to pasture his sheep upon a hill, and one day he saw something glittering on the opposite hill. So he went there to see what it was. It was a golden mortar. He took it up and said to his daughter, "I will give this mortar to our king."

But she said, "Don't do that. If you give him the mortar, you won't have the pestle, and he is sure to ask for it, and then you will get into trouble."

But the shepherd thought that she was only a silly girl. He took the mortar, and, when he came before the king, he said, "Begging your pardon, Mr. King, I want to give you this mortar."

The king answered him roughly, "If you give me the mortar, I must have the pestle as well. Unless the pestle is here within three days, your life will be forfeit."

The shepherd began to lament, "My daughter was right when she said that when you had got the mortar you would want the pestle too. I wouldn't listen to her, so it serves me right."

"Have you such a clever daughter as that?" asked the king.

"Indeed I have," said the shepherd.

"Then tell your daughter that I will marry her, if she comes neither walking nor riding, clothed nor unclothed, neither by day nor by night, neither at noon nor in the morning. And I won't ask for the pestle either."

The shepherd went home and said, "You can get me out of this, if you go to Mr. King neither walking nor riding, neither clothed nor unclothed, neither by day nor by night, neither at noon nor in the morning. If you can do this, he will marry you, and he will not ask for the pestle."

The daughter wasn't a bit frightened. She came with the fall of dusk (and that was neither at noon nor in the morning); she dressed herself in fishing-nets; she took a goat, and she partly rode on the goat and partly walked.

And when the king saw that she had only a fishing-net on, that she came with the approach of dusk, and that she was partly walking, partly riding a goat, he was bound to marry her. But he said to her, "You will be my wife so long as you don't give advice to anybody; for if you do, you must leave me."

Well, she didn't give advice to anybody until one day there was a market in the town, and a farmer's mare had a foal at the market. The foal ran away to another farmer, who was there with a gelding, and that farmer said, "This foal belongs to me."

They went to law about it, and at last the matter came before the king. And the king, considering that every animal ought to run to its mother, decided that a gelding had had a foal.

The farmer who owned the mare went down the stairs, saying over and over again, "The gelding has foaled! The gelding has foaled!"

The queen heard him, and she said, "Man, you are talking nonsense."

So he told her that he had been at the market and that his mare had foaled, but the foal ran to another farmer who was there with a gelding. "And now," he said, "it has been decided that the gelding has foaled." So he thought there could be no mistake; at any rate, he couldn't help it.

When the queen heard this story she said, "Tomorrow, my lord

the king will go out for a stroll. Take a fishing-net, and begin fishing on the road in front of him. The king will ask you, 'Why are you fishing on a dry road?' And you must answer, 'Why not? It's as hopeful as expecting a gelding to foal.' But you must not say who gave you this advice.''

So it was. As the king was walking along he saw the farmer fishing on the dry road. He asked him why he was fishing there.

''Why not?'' said he. ''It's as hopeful as expecting a gelding to foal.''

The king at once began to berate the farmer. ''That's not out of your own head,'' he said, and he kept at the farmer until he let the secret out.

So the king came home, summoned the queen, and said to her, ''You have been with me for a long time, but you have given advice in spite of all, so you must go tomorrow. But I will allow you to take with you the thing you like best.''

It was no good arguing. So the king invited all his courtiers and prepared a splendid banquet. When the banquet was finished, the queen said to the king, ''Before we part, you must drink this glass of wine to my health,'' and she had put some opium into the wine on the sly.

The king drank it at a draft and fell asleep at once. A carriage was got ready, and the queen put the king in it and drove to her father's old hut. There she laid the king on the straw, and when he woke up, he asked where he was.

"You are with me. Didn't you tell me that I could take the thing I liked best with me?"

The king saw how clever she was, and he said, "Now you can give advice to anybody you like."

And so they drove back home, and he was king and she was queen again.

Vassilissa Golden Tress,
Bareheaded Beauty

Russia

There once lived a Tsar Svaitozar. This Tsar had two sons and a beauty of a daughter. For twenty years she had lived in her bright chamber. The Tsar and Tsaritsa admired her, and so did the nurses and maidens; but not one of the princes and champions had seen her face. And this beauty was called Vassilissa Golden Tress.

She never left her chamber; she did not breathe the free air. She had many bright dresses and jewels, but was bored; it was dull for her in the chamber. Her robes were a burden, her thick golden silk hair, bound in a tress, was so long it fell to her feet, and people called her Vassilissa Golden Tress, Bareheaded Beauty. The kingdom was filled with her fame. Many Tsars heard of her and sent envoys to Tsar Svaitozar to beat the ground with their foreheads and ask for her hand in marriage.

The Tsar was in no hurry, but when the time came, he sent messengers to all lands with tidings that Vassilissa would choose a bridegroom; and inviting suitors to assemble and collect at his palace to feast, he himself went to the lofty chamber to tell Vassilissa the Beautiful. She was glad in her heart. Looking out of the sloping window from behind the golden lattice, she saw the green garden, the flowery meadow, and she was eager to walk there; she asked him to let her go out to the garden to play with the maidens. "My sovereign father," she said, "I have not seen God's world yet. I have not walked on the grass, or smelled the flowers; I have not seen your palace. Let me go with my nurses and maidens to walk in the garden."

The Tsar permitted it, and Vassilissa the Beautiful went down from the lofty chamber to the broad court. The plank gate was open, and she entered the green meadow. In front was a steep mountain;

on that mountain stood windswept trees; on the meadow were beautiful flowers of many kinds. Vassilissa, picking blue flowers, stepped aside a little from her nurses; there was no caution in her young mind; her face was exposed, her beauty uncovered. Suddenly a mighty whirlwind rose, such as had not been seen, heard of, or remembered by old people; the whirlwind turned and twisted, and behold! It seized Vassilissa and carried her through the air.

The nurses screamed and shrieked; they ran and stumbled, threw themselves on every side; they saw nothing but how the whirlwind shot away with her. And Vassilissa Golden Tress was borne over many lands, across deep rivers, through three kingdoms into the fourth, into the dominions of the Savage Serpent.

The nurses hurried to the palace, covering themselves with tears, and threw themselves at the feet of the Tsar. "Sovereign, it's not our fault. Please don't kill us, but let us speak. The whirlwind bore away our sun, Vassilissa Golden Tress, the Bareheaded Beauty, and we don't know where."

The Tsar was sad, he was angry; but despite his anger he pardoned the poor women.

Next morning the princes and kings' sons came to the Tsar's palace, and seeing the sadness and seriousness of the Tsar they asked him what had happened.

"There is a sin to my account," said the Tsar. "My dear daughter, Vassilissa Golden Tress, has been borne away by the whirlwind, I know not whither," and he told everything as it had happened.

Talk rose among the guests, and the princes and kings' sons thought and talked among themselves. "Perhaps the Tsar is refusing us. This may be a story to prevent us from seeing his daughter." They searched Vassilissa's chamber; but nowhere did they find her.

The Tsar gave presents to each one from his treasure. They mounted their steeds, he did them honor; the bright guests took their leave, and went to their own lands.

The two young Tsareviches, brave brothers of Vassilissa Golden Tress, seeing the tears of their father and mother, begged of their parents, "Let us go, our father – bless us, our mother – to find your daughter, our sister."

"My dear sons, my own children," said the Tsar, without joy, "where will you go?"

"We will go, Father, everywhere – where a road lies, where a bird flies, where our eyes lead us; maybe we shall find her."

The Tsar gave his blessing, the Tsaritsa prepared them for the journey; they wept, and they parted.

The two Tsareviches journeyed on. Whether the road would be near or far, long or short, they did not know. They traveled a year, they traveled two. They passed three kingdoms. Lofty, blue-tinged mountains could be seen; between these mountains were sandy plains: the land of the Savage Serpent. And the Tsareviches inquired of those whom they met had they not heard, had they not seen, where Vassilissa Golden Tress was. And from all the answer was the same: "We know not where she is, and we have not heard."

The Tsar's sons approached a great town. A decrepit old man stood on the road, crooked-eyed and lame, with a crutch and a bag, begging alms. The Tsareviches stopped, threw him a silver coin, and asked had he not seen, had he not heard of the Tsarevna Vassilissa Golden Tress, Bareheaded Beauty?

"Ah! My friend," said the old man, "it is clear that you are from a strange land. Our ruler, the Savage Serpent, has forbidden us strongly and sternly to speak with men from abroad. We are forbidden under penalty to tell or relate how a whirlwind bore the beautiful princess past the town."

Now the sons of the Tsar understood that their sister was near.

They urged on their restive steeds and approached the castle of gold which stood on a single pillar of silver; over the castle was a curtain of diamonds; the stairways, mother-of-pearl, opened and closed like wings.

At this moment Vassilissa the Beautiful was looking in sadness through the golden lattice, and she cried out for joy. She knew her brothers from a distance, just as if her heart had told her. And Vassilissa went down in silence to meet them, to welcome them to the castle; the Savage Serpent was absent.

Vassilissa the Beautiful was wary; she feared the serpent might see them. They had barely entered when the silver pillar groaned, the stairways opened, all the roofs glittered; the whole castle began to turn and move. Vassilissa was frightened, and said to her brothers, "The serpent is coming, the serpent is coming; that's why the castle goes round! Hide, brothers!"

She had barely said this when the Savage Serpent flew in, whistled with a hero's whistle and cried with a thundering voice, "What living man is here?"

"We, Savage Serpent," answered the Tsar's sons, without fear; "from our birthplace we've come for our sister."

"Oh, the young men are here!" shouted the serpent, clapping his wings. "You should not have sought death from me, nor traveled so far your sister to free; you think yourselves champions, I can see, but your strengths are puny compared to me." And the serpent caught one of them with his wing, struck him against his brother, whistled and shouted. The castle guard ran to him, took the dead Tsareviches, and threw them both down a deep ditch.

The Tsarevna Vassilissa Golden Tress wept bitterly, took neither food nor drink, would not look on the world. Two days and three passed. But she did not choose to die; it was not time for that. She took pity on her beauty and took counsel of her hunger. On the third day she ate, and, thinking how to free herself from the serpent, began to gain knowledge by wheedling.

"Savage Serpent," said she, "great is your power, mighty your flight; is it possible that you have no foe?"

"Not yet," replied the serpent; "it was fated at my birth that my foe should be Ivan Goroh [John Pea]; and he will be born from a pea."

The serpent said this in jest; he expected no foe. The strong one relied on his strength; but the jest came true.

The mother of Vassilissa Golden Tress was grieving because she had no news of her children after the Tsarevna and the Tsareviches were lost.

She went one day to walk in the garden with her ladies; the day was hot, she was thirsty. In that garden, from a foothill, spring water ran forth in a stream, and above it was a white marble well. They drew, with a golden cup, water pure as a tear. The Tsaritsa was eager to drink, and with the water she swallowed a pea. The pea burst, and the Tsaritsa became heavy; the pea increased and grew. In time the Tsaritsa gave birth to a son; they called him Ivan Goroh, and he grew, not by the year, but by the hour, smooth and plump; he became lively, laughed, jumped about, somersaulted on the sand, and his strength grew in him all the time, so that by the time he was ten years old he was a mighty champion. Then he asked the Tsar and Tsaritsa if he had had any brothers and sisters, and so he heard how the whirlwind had borne away his sister, it was not known where, and how his two brothers had begged to go in search of their sister, and were lost without tidings.

"Father, Mother," begged Ivan Goroh, "let me go too; give me your blessing to find my brothers and sister."

"What are you saying, my child?" asked the Tsar and Tsaritsa at once. "You are still green and young; your brothers went and were lost; if you go, you too will be lost."

"Perhaps I shall not be lost," said Ivan Goroh. "I want to find my brothers and sister."

The Tsar and Tsaritsa begged their dear son, but he craved, cried and entreated. They prepared him for the road and let him go with tears.

Ivan Goroh was free. He went out into the open field, traveled one day, traveled another. Toward night he came to a dark forest; in that forest was a cabin on hen's legs, trembling and turning in the wind. Ivan spoke the old saying, from his nurse's tale. "Cabin, cabin," said he, "turn your back to the forest, your front to me," and the cabin turned around to Ivan. Out of the window an old woman was looking, and she asked, "Whom is God bringing?"

Ivan bowed, and hastened to ask, "Have you not seen, Grandmother, in what direction the passing whirlwind carries beautiful maidens?"

"Oh, young man," said she, coughing, and looking at Ivan, "that whirlwind has frightened me too, so that I have sat in this cabin a hundred and twenty years, and I never go out! He might fly up and sweep me away. That's not a whirlwind, but the Savage Serpent."

"How could I find him?" asked Ivan.

"What are you thinking of, my world? The serpent will swallow you."

"Maybe he will not swallow me."

"Watch out, champion, or you will not save your head. But if you should come back, give me your word to bring from the serpent's castle the water with which, if a man sprinkles himself, he will grow young,'' said she, grinding her teeth.

"I will get it, Grandmother, I give you my word."

"I believe you, on your honor! Go straight to where the sun sets. In one year you will reach the bare mountain there; ask for the road to the serpent's kingdom."

"God save you, Grandmother!"

"There is no reason for thanks, Ivan Goroh."

Well, Ivan Goroh went to the land where the sun sets. A story is soon told, but a deed's not soon done. He passed three kingdoms, and went to the serpent's land; before the gates of the town he saw a beggar, a lame, blind old man with a crutch, and, giving him charity, he asked if the young Tsarevna Vassilissa Golden Tress was in that town.

"She is, but it is forbidden to say so," answered the beggar.

Ivan knew that his sister was there; the good, bold hero gathered his courage, and went to the palace. At that time Vassilissa Golden Tress was looking out of the window to see if the Savage Serpent was coming; and, seeing the young champion from afar and wishing to know about him, she sent quietly to learn from what land he had come, who he was, and if he came from her father or her mother.

Hearing that Ivan, her youngest brother, had come (for she did not know him by sight), Vassilissa ran to him and wet him with tears. "Run, brother, quickly!" cried she. "The serpent will soon be here; he will see you and destroy you."

"My dear sister," answered Ivan, "whoever asked me to flee, I should not listen. I have no fear of the serpent, no fear of his strength."

"But are you really Ivan Goroh?" asked Vassilissa Golden Tress. "Can you overcome him?"

"Wait, dear sister; first give me a drink. I have traveled in the heat, I am tired from the road; I want a drink."

"What will you drink, brother?"

"Three gallons of sweet mead, dear sister."

Vassilissa ordered a three-gallon measure of sweet mead, and Goroh drank it all at one breath. He asked for another; the Tsarevna looked at him in wonder, and ordered it.

"Well, brother, I did not know you; but now I believe that you are Ivan Goroh!"

"Let me sit down a moment to rest from the road."

Vassilissa commanded her servants to bring a strong chair; but the chair broke under Ivan, flew into bits. They brought another all bound with iron, and that one cracked and bent. "Oh, brother," cried Vassilissa, "that is the chair of the Savage Serpent!"

"Now it is clear that I am heavier than he," said Goroh, laughing.

He rose and went down the street, from the castle to the forge; there he ordered the serpent's blacksmith to forge him an iron club of nine tons' weight. The blacksmith hurried to his work. They hammered the iron; night and day the hammers thundered, the sparks flying. In forty hours the work was done. Fifty men were barely able to carry the club; but Ivan Goroh, seizing it in one hand, hurled the club to the sky: it flew, roaring like a storm, and whirled above the clouds, out of sight. All the people ran trembling with terror, thinking if that club were to fall on the town, it would break the walls and crush the people; if it fell in the sea, it would raise the sea and flood the town. But Ivan Goroh went quietly to the castle, saying they should tell him when the club was coming. All the people looked out for the club. "Isn't the club coming?" They waited an hour, they waited two; on the third hour they ran to say that the club was coming. Goroh ran to the square, put forth his hand, and caught the club as it came; he did not bend, but the iron bent on the palm of his hand. Ivan took the club, pressed it against his knee, straightened it, and went to the castle.

All at once a terrible whistling was heard. The Savage Serpent was racing on Whirlwind, his steed, flying like an arrow, breathing fire. The serpent had the body of a champion, but his head was the head of a serpent. When he flew, the whole castle quivered; when he approached, it began to whirl and dance. But now the castle was still: clearly someone was sitting inside. The serpent grew thoughtful, whistled, shouted; the whirlwind steed shook his dark mane, opened his broad wings, reared, and roared.

The serpent flew up to the castle, but the castle did not move. "Ho!" roared the Savage Serpent. "It is plain there is a foe. Is not Goroh at my house?" Out came the champion. "I'll put you on the palm of one hand, and slap you with the other, Ivan Goroh; they won't find your bones."

"We shall see," said Ivan Goroh.

The serpent cried from his whirlwind, "Prepare yourself."

"Prepare yourself, Savage Serpent," said Ivan, and raised his club.

The Savage Serpent flew up to strike Ivan, to pierce him with his spear, and missed. Goroh sprang to one side, and kept his balance.

"Now I'll finish you!" roared Goroh. Raising his club, he struck

the serpent a blow that tore him to pieces, scattered him; the club went across the earth, went through two kingdoms into a third.

The people hurled up their caps and saluted Ivan as their Tsar. But Ivan, seeing the wise blacksmith, thought to reward him for having made the club quickly, so he called up the old man and said to the people, "Here is your Tsar; obey his good commands, as before you obeyed the Savage Serpent's evil ones."

Ivan also took the water of life and the water of death, and sprinkled his brothers; they rose up, rubbed their eyes and thought, "We slept long; God knows what has happened."

"Without me you would have slept forever, my dear brothers," said Ivan Goroh, pressing them to him.

He did not forget to take the serpent's water; he made a ship, and sailed down the river with Vassilissa Golden Tress to his own land, through three kingdoms into the fourth. He did not forget the old woman in the cabin; he let her wash in the serpent's water. She turned into a young woman, began to sing and dance, ran out after Goroh, and showed him the road home.

His father and mother met him with joy and honor. They sent messengers to every land with tidings that their daughter Vassilissa had returned. In the town there was ringing, and in the ears triple ringing; trumpets sounded, drums were beaten, guns thundered.

A bridegroom came to Vassilissa, and brides were found for Ivan Goroh and his two brothers; they had eight crowns made, and celebrated four weddings.

The grandfathers of our grandfathers were there; they drank the mead, but by the time it reached us, it only wet our moustaches, and there was none to drink. And Ivan, after the death of his father, received the crown, and ruled the land with renown; and age after age the name of Goroh was famous.

How the Foolish Brother Was Drowned

Latvia

There were three brothers. Two of them were clever, but the third brother was a fool.

The fool annoyed the clever brothers, so they stuffed him into a leather sack and set out to a lake to drown him.

On the way, the brothers stopped at an inn for a drink. Left outside, the foolish brother writhed and moaned in the sack, crying out, "Dear God, what are they doing to me? They want to make me Tsar, though I can neither read nor write!"

At that moment, a certain lord was driving a herd of sheep and cattle past the inn. He heard what the fool said inside the sack, and said, "Come out! I will go instead of you. I can both read and write. I have always thought I would make an excellent Tsar."

So the lord opened the sack, let the fool out, and got in it himself. The fool fastened up the sack and went off with the sheep and cattle, while the lord lay quietly in the sack and thought about being Tsar.

At last the clever brothers came out of the inn and went on their way. They carried the sack to the lake, then threw it into the water through a hole in the ice.

On their way home, they passed the third brother, alive and unharmed, driving a herd of sheep and cattle. "Where did you get them?" they asked.

"I seized them in the lake, and brought home as many as I could; if you had sunk the sack deeper, I should have captured more," he replied.

"What does this mean?" the brothers said to each other. "If that fool was able to capture so many cattle, just think how many we could get, as clever as we are, if he threw us in." They considered a while, and said, "Brother, put us in sacks, carry us to the lake, and sink us in the deepest part."

The fool took the brothers, put each of them in a sack, and carried them to the lake.

Making a hole in the ice in the center of the lake, he cast in one of his brothers, who gurgled under the water. "What does he say?" asked the remaining brother.

"Oh, he is already driving the cattle," was the answer.

"Then throw me in quickly, so that he doesn't steal my portion of the herd!"

The fool threw in the second brother, and went home, and lived as the sole owner of his father's estate.

Cinder Jack

Hungary

A peasant had three sons. One morning he sent out the eldest to guard the vineyard. The lad went, and was cheerfully eating a cake he had taken with him, when a frog hopped up to him and asked him to let it have some of his cake. "Are you sure you don't want anything else?" asked the lad angrily, and picked up a stone to drive the frog away. The frog left without a word, and the lad soon fell asleep, and on waking, found the whole vineyard laid waste. The next day the father sent his second son into the vineyard, but he fared like the first.

The father was very angry about it, and did not know what to do. Then his youngest son spoke up, who was always sitting in a corner amongst the ashes, and was not thought fit for anything, and whom for this reason they nicknamed Cinder Jack. "My father, send me out, and I will take care of the vineyard." His father and his brothers laughed at him, but they allowed him to try his luck; so Cinder Jack went to the vineyard, and, taking out his cake, began to eat it. The frog again appeared and asked for a piece of cake, which Jack at once gave to it.

When they had finished their breakfast, the frog gave the lad a copper, a silver, and a gold rod, and told him that three horses would appear shortly, of copper, silver, and gold, and they would try to trample down the vineyard; but if he beat them with the rods the frog had given him, they would at once become tame, and be his servants, and could at any time be summoned to carry out his orders.

It happened as the frog foretold, and the vineyard produced a rich vintage. But Cinder Jack never told his father or his brothers how he had been able to preserve the vineyard; in fact, he kept it all a secret, and still spent his time as usual, lying about in his favorite corner.

One Sunday the king had a high fir-pole erected in front of the church, and a sprig of rosemary made of gold tied to the top, and promised his daughter's hand in marriage to the man who could take the rosemary down in one jump on horseback. All the knights of the realm tried their fortune, but not one of them was able to jump high enough. But all of a sudden a knight clad in copper mail, on a copper horse, appeared with his visor down, snatched the rosemary with an easy jump, and quickly disappeared. When his two brothers got home they told Cinder Jack what had happened, and he remarked that he had seen the whole proceeding much better than they, and on being asked "Where from?" his answer was, "From the top of the hoarding." His brothers had the hoarding pulled down at once, so that their younger brother might not look on anymore.

Next Sunday a still higher pole, with a golden apple at the top, was set up; and whosoever wished to marry the king's daughter had to take the apple down. Again, hundreds upon hundreds tried, but all in vain; till at last a knight in silver mail, on a silver horse, took it and disappeared. Cinder Jack again told his brothers that he saw the festivities much better than they did; he saw them, he said, from the pigsty; so this was pulled down also.

The third Sunday a silk kerchief interwoven with gold was displayed at the top of a still higher fir-pole, and once again nobody succeeded in getting it, until a knight in gold mail, on a gold horse, appeared, snatched it down, and galloped off. Cinder Jack again told his brothers that he had seen everything from the top of the

house; and his envious brothers had the roof of the house taken off, so that the youngest brother might not look on again.

The king, guessing that the copper, silver, and gold knights must be the same man, now had it announced that the knight who had shown himself worthy of his daughter should come forward, and should bring with him the golden rosemary, the apple, and the silk kerchief; but no one came. So the king ordered every man in the realm to appear before him, and still the knight in question could not be found; till, at last, he arrived clad in gold mail on a gold charger; whereupon the bells were at once rung, and hundreds and hundreds of cannons fired. The knight, having handed to the princess the golden rosemary, the apple, and the kerchief, respectfully asked for her hand, and, having obtained it, lifted his visor. The people, to their great astonishment, recognized Cinder Jack, whom they had forgotten even to ask into the king's presence.

The goodhearted lad had his brothers' house rebuilt, and gave them presents as well. He took his father to live with him, and as the old king died soon after, Cinder Jack became king in his turn. Cinder Jack is reigning still, and is respected and honored by all his subjects!

Goldenhair

Czechoslovakia

There was a king who was so clever that he understood all animals, and knew what they said to one another. Hear how he learnt it. Once upon a time there came to him a little old woman, who brought him a snake in a basket, and told him to have it cooked; if he dined off it, he would understand what any animal in the air, on the earth, or in the water said. The king liked the idea of understanding what nobody else understood, paid the old woman well, and forthwith ordered his servant to cook "the fish" for dinner. "But," said he, "be sure you don't take even a morsel of it on your tongue, else you shall pay for it with your head."

George, the servant, thought it odd that the king forbade him so sternly to do this. "In my life I never saw such a fish," said he to himself. "It looks just like a snake! And what sort of cook would it be who didn't take a taste of what he was cooking?" When it was cooked, he took a morsel on his tongue, and tasted it. Thereupon he heard something buzzing round his ears, "Some for us, too! Some for us, too!" George looked round, and saw nothing but some flies that were flying about in the kitchen. Again somebody called with a hissing voice in the street outside, "Where are you going? Where are you going?" And shriller voices answered, "To the miller's barley! To the miller's barley!" George peeped through the window, and saw a gander and a flock of geese. "Aha!" said he. "That's the

kind of fish it is." Now he knew what it was. He hastily thrust one more morsel into his mouth, and carried the snake to the king as if nothing had happened.

After dinner the king ordered George to saddle the horses and accompany him, as he wished to take a ride. The king rode in front and George behind. As they were riding over a green meadow, George's horse bounded and began to neigh, "Ho! Ho! Brother, I feel so light that I should like to jump over mountains!" "As for that," said the other, "I should like to jump about, too, but there's an old man on my back; if I were to skip, he'd tumble on the ground like a sack and break his neck." "Let him break it – what matter?" said George's horse. "Instead of an old man you'll carry a young one." George laughed heartily at this conversation, but so quietly that the king knew nothing about it. But the king, who also understood perfectly well what the horses were saying to each other, looked round, and seeing a smile on George's face, asked him what he was laughing at. "Nothing, your illustrious Majesty," said George in excuse, "only something just occurred to me." Nevertheless, the old king already suspected him; neither did he feel confidence in the horses, so he turned and rode back home.

When they arrived at the palace, the king ordered George to pour him out a glass of wine. "But your head for it," said he, "if you don't pour it full, or if you pour it so that it runs over." George took the decanter and poured. Just then in flew two birds through the window; one was chasing the other, and the one that was trying to get away carried three golden hairs in its beak. "Give them to me!" said the first. "They are mine." "I shan't; they're mine; I picked them up." "But I saw them fall, when the golden-haired maiden was combing her hair. At any rate, give me two." "Not one!" Hereupon the other bird made a rush, and seized the golden hairs. As they struggled for them in the air, one hair remained in each bird's beak, and the third golden hair fell on the ground, where it made a ringing sound. At this moment George looked round at it, and the wine overflowed. "You've forfeited your life!" shouted the king; "but I'll deal mercifully with you if you obtain the golden-haired maiden, and bring her to me as my wife."

What was George to do? If he wanted to save his life, he must go

in search of the maiden, though he did not know where to look for her. He saddled his horse, and rode at random. He came to a black forest, and there, under the trees by the roadside, a bush was burning; some cowherd had set it on fire. Under the bush was an anthill; sparks were falling on it, and the ants were fleeing in all directions with their little white eggs. "Help, George, help!" they cried mournfully. "We're being burnt to death, as well as our young ones in the eggs." He got down from his horse at once, cut away the bush, and put out the fire. "When you are in trouble think of us, and we'll help you."

He rode on through the forest, and came to a lofty pine. On the top of this pine was a raven's nest, and below, on the ground, were two young ravens crying and complaining, "Our father and mother have flown away; we've got to seek food for ourselves, and we poor little birds can't fly yet. Help us, George, help us! Feed us, or we shall die of hunger!" George did not stop long to consider, but jumped down from his horse, and thrust his sword into its side, that the young ravens might have something to eat. "When you are in need think of us, and we'll help you."

After this, George had to go on foot. He walked a long, long way through the forest, and when he at last got out of it, he saw before him a long and broad sea. On the shore of this sea two fishermen were quarreling. They had caught a large golden fish in their net, and each wanted to have it for himself. "The net is mine, so the fish is mine," said the first.

The other replied, "Much good would your net have been, if it hadn't been for my boat and my help."

"If we catch such another fish, it will be yours."

"Not so; you wait for the next, and give me this."

"I'll settle this," said George. "Sell me the fish – I'll pay you well for it – and you divide the money between you, share and share alike." He gave them all the money that the king had given him for his journey, leaving nothing at all for himself. The fishermen were delighted, and George let the fish go again into the sea. It splashed merrily through the water, dived, and then, not far from the shore, lifted up its head, saying, "When you want me, George, think of me, and I'll repay you." It then disappeared.

"Where are you going?" the fishermen asked George.

"I'm looking for the golden-haired maiden to be the bride of the old king, my lord, and I don't even know where to look for her."

"We can tell you all about her," said the fishermen. "It's Goldenhair, the king's daughter, of the Crystal Palace, on the island over there. Every day at dawn she combs her golden hair, and the bright gleam from it flashes over sky and over sea. If you wish it, we'll take you over to the island ourselves, as you settled our quarrel so nicely. But take care to bring away the right girl; there are twelve maidens – the king's daughters – but only one has golden hair."

When George was on the island, he went into the Crystal Palace to entreat its king to give the king, his lord, the golden-haired daughter to wife. "I will," said the king, "but you must earn her. You must in three days perform three tasks, which I shall set you, one each day. Meanwhile, you can rest till tomorrow."

Next day, early, the king said to him, "My Goldenhair had a necklace of costly pearls; the necklace broke, and the pearls were scattered in the long grass in the green meadow. You must collect all these pearls, without missing one." George went into the meadow; it was long and broad; he knelt on the grass, and began to search. He sought and sought from morn to noon, but never saw a pearl. "Ah! if my ants were here, they might help me."

"Here we are to help you," said the ants, running in every direction, but always crowding round him. "What do you want?"

"I have to collect pearls in this meadow, but I don't see one."

"Only wait a bit, we'll collect them for you." Before long they brought him a multitude of pearls out of the grass, and he had only to string them on the necklace. Afterward, when he was going to fasten up the necklace, one more ant limped up – it was lame, its foot had been scorched in the fire at the anthill – and cried out, "Stop, George, don't fasten it up; I'm bringing you one more pearl."

When George brought the pearls to the king, the king counted them over; not one was missing. "You have done your business well," said he. "Tomorrow I shall give you another task." In the morning George came, and the king said to him, "My Goldenhair was bathing in the sea, and lost a gold ring there; you must find it and bring it to me."

George went to the sea, and walked sorrowfully along the shore. The sea was clear, but so deep that he couldn't even see the bottom, much less could he seek and find the ring there. "Oh that my golden fish were here; it might be able to help me."

At that something glittered in the sea, and up swam the golden fish from the deep to the surface of the water. "Here I am to help you; what do you want?"

"I've got to find a gold ring in the sea, and I can't even see the bottom."

"I just met a pike which was carrying a gold ring in its mouth. Only wait a bit, I'll bring it to you." And soon it returned from the deep water and brought him the pike, ring and all.

The king commended George for doing so well, and then next

morning laid upon him the third task: "If you wish me to give your king my Goldenhair to wife, you must bring her the waters of death and of life; she will require them." George did not know where to find these waters, and went haphazardly hither and thither, wherever his feet carried him, till he came to a black forest. "Ah," he sighed, "if my young ravens were here, perhaps they would help me."

Now there was a rustling over his head, and two young ravens appeared above him. "Here we are to help you; what do you wish?"

"I've got to fetch the waters of death and of life, and I don't know where to look for them."

"Oh, we know them well; only wait a bit, we'll bring them to you."

After a short time they each brought George a bottle-gourd full of water; in the one gourd was the water of life, in the other the water of death. George was delighted with his good fortune, and hastened to the castle. At the edge of the forest he saw a cobweb extending from one pine tree to another; in the midst of the cobweb sat a large spider sucking a fly. George took the bottle with the water of death, sprinkled the spider, and the spider dropped to the ground like a ripe cherry – he was dead. He then sprinkled the fly with the water of life out of the other bottle, and the fly began to move, freed itself from the cobweb, and flew off into the air. "Lucky for you, George, that you've brought me to life again," it buzzed round his ears. "Without me you'd scarcely guess aright which of the twelve is Goldenhair."

When the king saw that George had completed this task also, he said he would give him his golden-haired daughter. "But," said he, "you must select her yourself." He then led him into a great hall, in the midst of which was a round table, and round the table sat twelve beautiful maidens, one like the other; but each had on her head a long kerchief reaching down to the ground, white as snow, so that it couldn't be seen what manner of hair any of them had. "Here are my daughters," said the king. "If you guess which of them is Goldenhair, you have won her, and can take her away at once; but if you don't guess right, she is not for you, and you must depart without her."

George was in the greatest anxiety; he didn't know what to do. Whereupon something whispered into his ear, "Buzz! Buzz! Go round the table, I'll tell you which is the one." It was the fly that George had restored with the water of life. "It isn't this maiden – nor this – nor this; this is Goldenhair!"

"Give me this one of your daughters," cried George. "I have earned her for my lord."

"You have guessed right," said the king; and the maiden at once rose from the table, threw off her kerchief, and her golden hair flowed in streams from her head to the ground, and it gleamed and shone like the sun rising in the morning, so that George's eyes were dazzled.

Then the king gave his daughter all that was fitting for her journey, and George took her away to be his lord's bride. The old king's eyes sparkled, and he jumped for joy, when he saw Goldenhair, and he gave orders at once for preparations to be made for the wedding. "I intended to have you hanged for your disobedience, that the ravens might devour you," said he to George, "but you have served me so well that I shall only have your head cut off with an axe, and then I shall have you honorably buried." When George had been executed, Goldenhair begged the old king to grant her the body of his dead servant, and the king couldn't deny his golden-haired bride anything. She then fitted George's head to his body, and sprinkled him with the water of death, and the body and head grew together so that no mark of the wound remained. Then she sprinkled him with the water of life, and George rose up again, as if he had been born anew, as fresh as a stag, and youth beamed from his countenance.

"Oh, how heavily I have slept!" said George, and rubbed his eyes.

"Yes, indeed, you have slept heavily," said Goldenhair; "and if it hadn't been for me, you wouldn't have waked forever and ever."

When the old king saw that George had come to life again, and that he was younger and handsomer than before, he wanted to be made young again also. He gave orders at once that his head should be cut off, and that he should be sprinkled with the water. They cut his head off and sprinkled him with the water of life, till they'd sprinkled it all away; but his head wouldn't grow onto the body. Then, and not till then, did they begin to sprinkle him with the water of death, and in an instant the head grew onto the body; but the king was dead all the same, because they had no more of the water of life to bring him to life again. And since the kingdom couldn't be without a king, and they'd no one else so intelligent as George, who could understand all the animals, they made George king and Goldenhair queen.

Cinder-Stick

Georgia

There was once upon a time a young married couple. But the husband was lazy; he did nothing and refused to work. He sat all day long by the fireside, with a little stick in his hand with which he poked about among the ashes. That is why he was called Cinder-Stick.

"Husband!" said his wife one day. "Get up and stir yourself! Go out and work and bring something into the house! If you do not, then I cannot stay with you."

That did no good. He still went on sitting beside the fire, and would not stir outside the house. But on Easter Sunday he made up his mind to go to church. When he came home again he found the door locked against him, and his wife refused to let him in. So he asked her to give him a bagful of ashes, an awl, and a fresh cheese, and then slouched lazily away.

We do not know whether he went far or not. But at last he came to a broad river and saw, sitting on the opposite bank, a giant Div drinking greedily from the river.

Cinder-Stick got very frightened, but what could he do? There were only two things open to him, either to go home to his wife, or to stay and be eaten for breakfast by the Div. He thought it over, up and down, and round about. And this was the plan he finally thought out. He made a hole in his sack of ashes, then swung it quickly round and round his head, raising a tremendous cloud of dust.

The Div was astonished; he was even alarmed. He took up a stone, and told Cinder-Stick, "I bet you can't squeeze water out of a stone."

"Easy," said Cinder-Stick, and he took his new cheese, pretending it was a stone, and squeezed it as hard as he could, so that water ran out of it.

Then Cinder-Stick called across to the Div, "Listen to me! Come over here and let me climb up on your shoulders, so you can carry me across the river. I don't want to get my feet wet!"

The Div obeyed. When Cinder-Stick got up on his shoulder, the Div said, "Oh! How light you are!"

"That is because I am holding on to heaven with one hand," said Cinder-Stick. "If I let go, you will not be able to carry me."

"Let me see," said the Div. "Let go of heaven!"

Cinder-Stick took his awl and began to bore it into the Div's head. The Div began to roar, and told him to catch hold of heaven again.

When they got to the far bank, the Div said, "Now get down. It's time for a meal."

Cinder-Stick was terrified, but what could he do? He had to get down and accompany the Div home.

The Div's house pleased Cinder-Stick very much. There was an enormous loaf of bread in the oven. "Watch that loaf for me, and see it doesn't burn," said the Div. "I must prepare the dinner."

When Cinder-Stick saw that one side of the loaf was well browned, he wanted to turn it over. As he struggled with it, he slipped and fell beneath the loaf. He pushed with all his strength, but the loaf was too heavy, and he could not get out from underneath it. At length, the other Divs came home. When they saw him lying there under the loaf, they were astonished, and asked him what he was doing there,

"I had a dreadful pain in my stomach," answered Cinder-Stick,

"and so I laid the warm loaf on it to make it better. I feel much better now, so you can take the loaf away!"

Then the Divs wanted wine for dinner. One of them took a huge jug, gave it to Cinder-Stick, and said, "Here, be a good fellow! Outside in the courtyard you will find a wine barrel. Go and bring some wine!"

Cinder-Stick was frightened when he saw the huge jug, but he took it and went outside. The Divs waited and waited for his return, but as he never came they went out to see what had happened. There stood Cinder-Stick, spade in hand, about to dig out the wine barrel, which was bigger than a man, and sunk half its height in the ground.

"What on earth are you doing?" they asked

"Oh, it will be much easier to fetch the whole barrel," he replied. "What's the use of my running backwards and forwards with that little jug?"

Now the Divs began to get alarmed. "If nine of us can hardly move that wine barrel empty, and he alone is going to bring it in full, there is something strange about it," they said; and they filled the jug themselves and sat down to dinner. But when one of them coughed, his cough blew Cinder-Stick right up to the ceiling. The Divs looked up at him in astonishment, as he clung there to a rafter.

"What are you doing up there?" they asked him.

"How dare you cough in my presence?" he answered. "I will pull this stick out of the roof and warm your flanks with it!"

The Divs became more and more frightened. "Nine of us together can hardly move one of these rafters," they said among themselves, "and he calls it merely a stick!" They were so frightened that they fled the house and scattered in all directions. And Cinder-Stick settled down comfortably in the house they had forsaken.

One of the Divs, on his flight, met a fox, who asked him, "Where are you running to, Div? What has happened?"

"What? Where am I running to?" said the Div. "Away, that's where! A man has come to our house and nearly swallowed us all up!"

But the fox laughed out loud when the Div told him the whole story. "Why, that is Cinder-Stick, a poor, starving wretch!" he said. "His wife drove him out of the house because of his laziness. I know them both quite well. I have eaten many of their hens. Fancy you being frightened of that miserable creature!"

"You haven't seen him," said the Div. "I don't believe you."

"Come along then! I'll show you. Follow me!" And the fox led the Div back to the house.

When Cinder-Stick saw them coming, he was frightened at first, but then he took courage, and began to shout at the fox. "You wretch!" he raged. "I told you to catch me twelve Divs, and here you bring me just one! You wait till I get hold of you!"

The Div didn't stop to hear any more. He was so terrified he ran away till he had put nine mountains between himself and Cinder-Stick.

Cinder-Stick took everything that belonged to the Divs, loaded it on camels, and set off back to his wife. She was pleased to see him with his booty, and they lived happily ever after.

The Useless Wagoner

Hungary

There was once in the world a king, and he had a Useless Wagoner who never and never did anything but frolic in the tavern. The whole standing day and all the ocean-great night there was nothing for him but singing and dancing, eating and drinking. He thought, "There's no need to work. The king has money enough, and to spare!"

But the king began to grow tired of this behavior. He called up the Useless Wagoner, and gave him a terrible scolding. But it is vain to seat a dog at table, and when the devil gets into a man he stays there; so it was labor lost to drive the Useless Wagoner to work, for he went his way, and frolicked as before. At last the king resolved to take his life, and calling him up, said, "Do you hear me, work-shy Useless Wagoner? You hopeless son of a no-good mother! If within the turn of four and twenty hours you do not make for me a three-hundred-gallon cask, without one joint or seam, I'll impale you on a stake."

The Useless Wagoner said not a word to all this, but put a hamper on his back, took a cutting-axe in his hand, and strolled off to the forest to find a tree fit to make a three-hundred-gallon cask.

When he came to the forest, being hungry and tired, he sat down under a large shady tree, opened his hamper, and began to eat lunch. He ate and ate till all at once, from some corner or another, a little fox stood before him and begged food to eat.

"Of course I'll give you something. The food came here, it will stay here." With that he threw a slice of bread and a bit of sausage to the fox.

When the fox had finished eating she said, "Are you listening, Useless Wagoner? As you have taken pity on me, I will take pity on you; one good turn deserves another. Though you have not told me, still I know why you have come to this forest. I know, too, that the king is scheming to kill you; but he'll not manage this time, for I

99

will help you out of your trouble and make you the three-hundred-gallon cask. And though one seam or joint is not much, even that will not be in it. Now lie down and rest.''

And so it was. The Useless Wagoner lay down and rested. Meanwhile the little fox got such a three-hundred-gallon cask ready, that although one joint or seam is not much, even that was not to be seen in it.

When the cask was finished, the Useless Wagoner took it home and gave it to the king, who, after looking at it, dropped his eyes and his lip like a sheep; for neither his father, his grandfather, nor his great-grandfather had ever seen such a cunningly made cask; not for gold could a seam or a joint be seen in it.

Well and good for the moment; but soon the king summoned the Useless Wagoner to his presence again, and cried out, ''Do you hear me, work-shy Useless Wagoner? Curses on you if within the turn of

four and twenty hours you do not make for me a chariot which will go by itself, without horses. I'll break you on a wheel!"

The Useless Wagoner said nothing, but put his hamper on his back, took his cutting-axe in his hand, and wandered off to the forest to find a tree fit to make a chariot.

When he came to the forest he was hungry, and tired too; therefore he sat down under a large, shady tree, opened his hamper, and began to eat lunch.

He ate and ate till all at once, from some corner or another, the little fox stood before him again, and begged food to eat.

"Of course, my dear little fox, I'll give you something. It came here, and it will stay here."

With that he threw a piece of bread and a slice of ham to the little fox, who after she had eaten, said, "Well, Useless Wagoner, one good turn deserves another. Though you have not told me, still I know why you are here. I know, too, that the king is scheming to kill you; but he won't this time, for I shall help you out of trouble. I'll make the chariot which will go by itself, without horses, for you; you lie down and rest."

And so it was. The Useless Wagoner lay down his head to rest; and meanwhile the little fox fashioned a beautiful chariot.

When all was ready, she roused the Useless Wagoner and said, "Here is the chariot which runs by itself; you have but to step in and command it to stop in the king's courtyard. And remember this: Here is a whistle that will serve you; should you fall into trouble, just blow; it will help you."

The Useless Wagoner thanked the fox for her kindness, and entered the chariot, which did not stop till it reached the king's courtyard.

When the king saw the chariot he said nothing, but shook his head, turned on the Useless Wagoner in a rage, and cried, "Useless Wagoner, devil take you! In my stable there are a hundred hares; and if you do not herd them for five days, if you do not drive them afield in the morning and bring them back at night so that not one shall be missing from the hundred, I'll strike off your head."

What was the poor Useless Wagoner to do? Against his will, because he had to, he led the hundred hares out of the stable and drove them afield. They had barely touched the edge of the field when they ran in as many directions as there were hares. Who could bring them together again? The poor Useless Wagoner ran first after one and then after another hare; he chased the whole day, but could not bring back a single hare. It was already growing late, time to go home, but the hundred hares were in a hundred places; therefore the Useless Wagoner became terribly sad, and wished to make an end of his own life; it was all the same whether he or the king took it; there was no salvation for him anyhow. So he put his hand in his bosom to take out his clasp-knife and strike himself in the heart, but instead of the knife he found the whistle which the little fox had given him. That was all he wanted; he drew out the whistle, sounded it, and behold! All the hares ran up to him, as tame as pet lambs fed from the palm of the hand.

When all the hares had come together he drove them home.

The king stood at the gate and let them in singly, counting, "One, two, three... ninety-nine, one hundred." Not one was missing.

Next day the Useless Wagoner drove the hares out again, and when they had barely touched the edge of the field they ran off in as many directions as there were hares.

But this time the Useless Wagoner took no thought of running and chasing after them; he thought to himself that he could take his whistle and blow, and they would come. So he lay down in a nice shady place, and slept to his liking.

But the king did not sleep; he was racking his brain to destroy the Useless Wagoner. So he called his only and dearly beloved daughter, and said to her, "My darling daughter, I have a great favor to ask of you."

"What may it be, my father the king?"

"Truly, nothing but this: that you dress in peasant's clothes, and go out to the field where the Useless Wagoner is herding the hundred hares, and beg one of him. If he will not give it for a good word, perhaps he will give it for a sweet kiss; but do not come home to me without the hare, even if he asks a piece of your body for it."

The princess granted her father's request. She gathered her wits about her, dressed up in peasant's clothes, and went in the field to the Useless Wagoner, who was sleeping at his leisure under a shady tree. The princess kicked him; he woke, and saw in a moment with whom he had to deal.

"God give you a good day, hareherd!"

"God save you, king's daughter! What good do you bring the poor hareherd?"

"I have brought nothing. I have come because I would like to get one little hare. Would you not sell me one for good money?"

"High princess, I will not sell one for money; but if you will give me three kisses, and I can give them back, then I don't mind; I'll give you a hare."

So the princess got a hare for three pairs of kisses, and ran home very joyfully; but just as she was touching the latch to open the gate, the hareherd sounded his whistle; the hare jumped like lightning from her bosom, and did not stop till it reached the flock.

The hareherd drove home his flock; the king was waiting for him at the gate, and let them in one by one, counting till he came to a hundred.

Next day the hareherd drove out his hares the third time, and left them to go their way.

The king now called his wife to the white chamber, and said to her, "My heart's beautiful love, I have a great favor to ask of you."

"And what may it be, my dear husband?"

"Truly, nothing but this: that you dress in peasant's clothes, go to the hareherd in the field, and ask a hare of him. If he will not give it for fair words, he may for a sweet kiss; but do not come home to me without a hare, even if he asks a piece of your flesh."

Well, the queen yielded to her husband's request, put on a peasant's dress, and went to the field, where she found the Useless Wagoner sleeping in the shade. She roused him with her foot; he knew at once who was in the peasant's dress.

"God give you a good day, hareherd!"

"God save you, kind queen! What good have you brought the poor hareherd? Why have you come, may I ask?"

"I have only come to ask if you will give me a hare for good money."

"I will not give a hare for money, my queen; but if you will give me three kisses, I will return them again. Then I don't mind; I'll risk my head, and let you have a hare."

So the queen got a hare for three pairs of kisses, and took her way home joyously; but just as she was putting her hand on the latch to open the gate, the hareherd sounded the whistle; the hare jumped like a flash from the queen's bosom, and did not stop till it joined its companions.

When the hares were all together, the hareherd drove them home. The king was waiting for him at the gate, and let each in singly, counting till he reached a hundred, not one missing from the round number.

The next time the king put on a peasant's dress, and went to the field himself. When he came to the hareherd he said, "God give you a good day!"

"God save you, poor man!" answered the hareherd. "What are you looking for?"

"Well, what's the use in delay or denial? I have come to buy a little hare of you for good money. Of course you will part with one."

"I will not give one for money; but if I can wear out twelve rods on your back, I don't mind; I'll risk my head on it."

What was the king to do? He stretched himself out with face and hands on the grass, and the hareherd flogged him as a corporal does a soldier; but he endured it all, gritting his teeth, and thinking to

himself, "Wait a bit, thief of a Useless Wagoner, you will have a dose when I get at you!"

But all to no use, for when the king had reached home, and was just putting his hand on the latch to open the gate, the whistle sounded, and the hare sprang away from him like a flash, and ran till it joined the flock.

Then the Useless Wagoner drove home the hundred hares a fourth time. The king was standing at the little gate; he counted them one by one, but could find no fault, for they were all there.

The Useless Wagoner drove out the hares the fifth time to pasture; but the king mounted the chariot which went wherever the owner commanded, and drove to the Useless Wagoner, taking three empty bags with him. "Do you hear me, you this-and-that-kind-of-work-shy hareherd! If you do not fill these three bags with truth, I will strike off your head."

To all this the Useless Wagoner answered with the words, "The king's daughter came out; I gave her, and she gave me. The queen came; I gave her, and she gave me. The king came; I gave him, and he –"

"Stop! Stop!" cried the king. "The three bags are full; and I'd rather be in hell than hear your words."

At this speech the chariot started off with the king, and never stopped till it took him to the bottom of hell.

Then the Useless Wagoner went home, married the king's daughter, became king, and reigns yet with his queen, unless he is dead.

The Longed-for Hedgehog
Poland

A childless woman once saw a hedgehog and said, "If only God would let me have this hedgehog to be my child." The wish was heard, and both the woman and her husband rejoiced, for the hedgehog made himself useful by carrying food to the father in the field. He also helped the mother by taking care of the pigs and driving them into the forest, where he remained six years. He used to sit there under a mushroom or a fern.

Once the king lost his way, and the hedgehog offered to direct him, if he would give his daughter to the hedgehog as a wife. The king thought to satisfy him with an empty promise, but the hedgehog demanded a written undertaking and the king's handkerchief with the royal name upon it. The king granted the request, but thought that none of his three daughters would accept the suitor.

After some weeks the hedgehog drove home the herd (which by this time had increased greatly) and begged his father to fasten a saddle and bridle to a cock, as he was departing into the world, but exactly where he was going he would not say.

The hedgehog rode to the royal castle, and showed his certificate and the handkerchief. The guards did not want to let him in, but they could not deny the royal name on the handkerchief. So the hedgehog rode the cock into the palace.

The king summoned his two older daughters, but neither of them would accept the visitor as a husband. The king called an armed force to kill the hedgehog, but the latter had a pipe, and when he blew upon it a still greater army of hedgehogs came and occupied the neighborhood. The king was at a loss how to proceed, when the youngest princess offered herself; whereupon the marriage took place and the hedgehog rode by her side in a carriage.

The next morning the princess found a handsome youth beside

her, and all rejoiced to see him. The hedgehog army now appeared as men, and the transformed prince, having sent for his parents, became king.

The Golden Apples and the Nine Peahens

Bulgaria

There was once upon a time an emperor who had three sons, and in his yard a golden apple tree, which flowered and bore fruit every night; but somebody stole the apples, and the emperor was utterly unable to discover who the robber was.

Once he was talking with his sons, and said to them, "I do not know where the fruit from our apple tree goes."

Then the eldest son answered him, "I will watch tonight to see who takes it."

When it became dark, the eldest son did as he had said. He went out and lay down under the tree.

Well, when the apples began to ripen in the course of the night, slumber overtook him, and he fell asleep; and when he awoke at dawn he looked – but where were the apples? Taken away!

When he saw this, he went and told everything to his father, just as it really happened.

Then the second son said to his father, "I will go tonight to watch, to see who takes the fruit." But, like his brother, about the time when the apples began to ripen, he fell asleep. When he woke up in the morning, where were the apples? Taken away!

Now came the turn of the third and youngest brother. He went out at dusk and placed a couch under the apple tree, lay down, and went to sleep. About midnight, when the apples began to ripen, he woke up and looked at the apple tree. It lit up the whole yard with the brightness of its fruit.

Just then, up flew nine golden peahens, eight of which settled upon the apple tree. The ninth landed on the ground beside his couch, and at once became a girl, who shone with beauty like a bright sun.

The youngest brother and the girl talked together while the other eight peahens were rifling the tree. When dawn came, she thanked him for the apples, and he begged her to leave just one behind her. She gave him two – one for himself, and one to take to his father; transformed herself into a peahen, and flew away, followed by the other eight.

In the morning the prince rose up and took one apple to his father, who was beside himself with joy, and showered him with praise.

The next evening the youngest prince went out again to watch the apple tree. In the morning he again brought his father an apple.

After a few days, his brothers began to envy him, because they had failed, and he had not. As evening approached, when the youngest prince was about to go out to watch the apple tree, his brothers sent an accursed witch to steal out and conceal herself behind his couch. The prince came, lay down without knowing that the old woman was behind his couch, and went to sleep as before.

About midnight, when the prince had just woken up, the nine peahens arrived; eight of them settled on the tree. The other landed on the ground beside his couch, transformed herself into the girl, and spoke with him.

While they were talking, the accursed old witch softly raised herself up and cut off a piece of the girl's long hair. At once the girl sprang aside, transformed herself into a peahen, and flew away, with the other eight behind her.

On seeing this, the prince leaped from his couch, shouting, "What's going on?" He soon spied the old woman behind the couch, and seized her. "Curses on you," he said. "You have done me an evil turn."

But the peahens came no more to the apple tree, which made the prince very sad. Day after day he wept and mourned. At last he determined to go to seek them all over the world, and went and told his father his intention. His father tried to comfort him, and said, "Stay, my son! I will find you another girl in my empire, as beautiful as you could wish for." But in vain; the son would not follow his father's advice, and made preparations to go. Taking with him one of his servants, he went into the world to find the peahens.

When he had traveled a long time, he came to a lake, in the midst of which was a rich palace, where lived an aged empress and her one daughter. The prince went to the old empress and asked her to tell him about the nine peahens, if she knew about them; and the old woman replied that she did, and that the nine peahens came daily to bathe in the lake.

She counseled him, "Never mind those nine peahens, my son. I have a handsome daughter, and abundance of wealth – it could all be yours." But as soon as the prince heard where the peahens were, he would not listen to her talk. In the morning he ordered his servant to get the horses ready to go to the lake.

Before they started, the old woman called the servant, bribed him, and gave him a little whistle, saying, "When it is time for the peahens to come to the lake, blow the whistle behind your master's neck; he will immediately fall asleep, and will not see them."

The accursed servant hearkened to her, took the whistle, and did as the old woman told him. When they arrived at the shore of the lake, he calculated the time when the peahens would arrive, and he blew the whistle behind his master's neck. The prince immediately fell as sound asleep as if he were dead.

Scarcely had he fallen asleep, when the peahens arrived; eight of them settled on the lake, and the ninth perched upon his horse. She began to try to awaken him, calling, "Arise, my birdie! Arise, my lamb! Arise, my dove!" But he heard nothing, and slept on as if dead.

When the peahens had finished bathing, they all flew away. The prince awoke, and asked his servant, "What has happened? Did they come?"

The servant replied, "They did come," and told him how eight of them had settled on the lake, and the ninth on his horse, and that she had tried to wake him. When the unhappy prince heard this from his servant, he was ready to kill himself from pain and anger.

The next morning they visited the shore of the lake again, but the accursed servant calculated the time to blow the whistle behind his master's neck, and the prince immediately fell asleep as if he were dead. Scarcely had he fallen asleep, when the nine peahens arrived; eight settled on the lake, and the ninth on his horse. She began to try to awaken him, calling, "Arise, my birdie! Arise, my lamb! Arise, my dove!" But he slept on as if he were dead, hearing nothing.

When he failed to awaken, and the peahens were about to fly away again, the one that had been trying to wake him turned and said to his servant, "When your master wakes, tell him that tomorrow it will be possible for him to see us here once more, but after that, never more." On saying this she took flight, and the others followed.

Scarcely had they flown away, when the prince awoke, and asked his servant, "Did they come?"

He told him, "They did come, and eight of them settled on the lake and the ninth on your horse, and she tried to wake you, but you slept soundly. As she departed, she told me to tell you that you will see her here once again tomorrow, and never more." When the prince heard this, he was ready to kill himself in his unhappiness, and did not know what to do for sorrow.

On the third day he got ready to go to the lake, mounted his horse, went to the shore, and, in order not to fall asleep, kept his horse continually in motion. But the wicked servant, as he followed his master, calculated the time, and blew the whistle behind his neck. The prince immediately leaned forward on his horse and fell asleep.

As soon as he was asleep, the nine peahens flew up; eight settled on the lake, and the ninth on his horse, and she endeavored to wake him, calling, "Arise, my birdie! Arise, my lamb! Arise, my dove!" But he slept as if he were dead, and heard nothing.

Then, when the peahens were about to fly away again, the one that had perched on his horse turned round, and said to his servant, "When your master wakes up, tell him to follow the sun to find me." Then she flew off, and those from the lake after her.

When they had flown away, the prince awoke, and asked his servant, "Did they come?"

He replied, "They did; and the one that perched on your horse told me to tell you to follow the sun to find her. But do not do so, master. Stay with the old empress and marry her daughter. See, she gave me this whistle to send you to sleep and save you from yourself."

"Curses on you," said the prince. "You have done me an evil turn."

113

Then he set off once more in search of the nine peahens. When he had traveled a long time, he came at dusk to the cottage of a hermit, and lodged there for the night. In the evening the prince asked the hermit, "Grandfather, have you heard of nine golden peahens?"

The hermit answered, "Yes, my son; you are fortunate in having come to me to ask about them. They are not far from here. It is not more than half a day's journey."

In the morning, the prince made ready to depart. The hermit came out to say farewell, and told him, "Go to the right, and you will find a large gate. When you enter that gate, turn once more to the right, and the road will lead you through their town to their palace."

He went on his way according to the hermit's words, until he came to the gate; then he turned to the right. Before long he came to the palace of the nine peahens. At the palace gate a watchman stopped him and asked his business. The prince told him all, where he had come from and who he was. After this the watchman went off to announce him to the empress.

When she heard who was there, the empress, who was none other than the ninth peahen, ran breathless through the palace. She stood before him in the form of a girl and, taking him by the hand, led him upstairs. Then the two rejoiced together, and in a day or two were wedded.

A few days after their marriage, the empress departed on a journey, and the prince remained alone. When she was about to set out, she gave him the keys of twelve cellars, and said to him, "You may open all the other cellars, but do not try any foolishness with the twelfth." Then she went away.

When the prince was alone in the palace, he thought to himself, "What does this mean, that I am to open all the other cellars, but not the twelfth? Glory to the Lord God! What can be in it?"

He then began to open the cellars one after the other. He came to the twelfth, and at first would not open it; but as he had nothing else to do, he began to brood and to ask himself, "What can be in this cellar, that she should tell me not to open it?"

At last he opened this one too, and found standing in the midst of it a cask bound with iron hoops, from which a voice could be heard, saying, "I am thirsty; I pray you, brother, give me a cup of water."

The prince took a cup of water, and sprinkled it on the bung of the cask; and as soon as he had done so, one of the hoops of the cask burst. He did it again, and another hoop burst. The voice then cried, "I am thirsty; brother, give me one more cup of water." The prince took another cup of water and poured it on the bung; and when he had finished, the third hoop of the cask burst, the cask split asunder, and out of it raged a dragon.

The dragon flew off on a mighty steed and, finding the empress on the road, seized her.

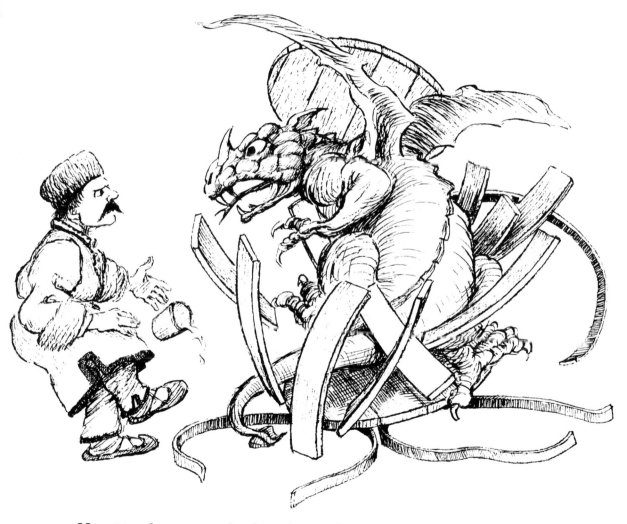

Her attendants came back to the castle and told their master that a dragon had carried the empress away. So once more he set off to seek her through the world.

When he had traveled a long time, he came to a marsh, and in that marsh he saw a little fish, which was trying to jump into the water but was unable to do so. This little fish addressed itself to the prince. "I pray you, brother, do me a good turn. Throw me into the water. I shall sometime be of use to you; only take a scale from me, and when you need me, rub it between your fingers."

On hearing this, the prince took a scale off the fish, and threw the fish into the water. He put the scale into a handkerchief and went on his way.

When he had gone a little farther, he saw a fox caught in a trap. The fox called out, "I pray you, brother, let me out of this trap; I shall someday be of use to you; only take one or two hairs from my fur, and when you need me, rub them between your fingers."

The prince let the fox out of the trap, took one or two hairs from it, and went on his way.

Thus he proceeded onward, till he came to a hill, and found a crow caught in a trap just like the fox before. As soon as the crow saw him, it cried out, "I pray you, be a brother to me, traveler, and let me out of this trap. I shall someday be of use to you; only take a feather or two from me, and when you need me, rub them between your fingers."

The prince took one or two feathers from the crow, let it out of the trap, and then went on his way.

As he went on in search of the empress, he met a man, and asked him, "I pray you, brother, do you know where the palace of the dragon emperor is?" The man showed him the way.

The prince thanked him, and went on, until he came to the palace of the dragon emperor. There he found his beloved, all alone, and when she saw him and he saw her, they were both full of joy. They began to plan together how to escape and soon saddled their horses, mounted, and galloped away.

When they had ridden off, the dragon came home and found the empress gone. "Now what shall we do?" said the dragon to his horse. "Shall we eat and drink, or pursue them?"

The horse replied, "Don't trouble yourself; eat and drink."

When he had dined, the dragon mounted his horse and galloped after the prince and the empress, and soon overtook them. He seized the empress, but said to the prince, "Go in safety. This time you are forgiven, because you gave me water in the cellar; but do not come a second time if your life is dear to you."

The poor prince remained behind, thunderstruck, and even turned his horse for home, and proceeded a little way. But he could not overcome his heart, and so he returned to the dragon's palace.

There he found the empress weeping. The prince told her, "When the dragon comes, ask him from whom he bought that horse, and tell me, so I may obtain one like it, and then we may escape." Then he went out, so that the dragon might not find him there.

When the dragon came, the empress began to coax him and make herself agreeable to him. She said to him, "What a swift horse yours is! From whom did you buy him? Tell me, I pray you."

He answered, "Such a horse cannot be bought. On a certain hill lives an old woman who has twelve horses in her stable, all so magnificent that each one is better than the next. The one in the corner looks skinny, but he is the best of all, and is the brother of mine; he could fly to the sky. Whoever seeks to obtain a horse from the old woman must serve her three days. The old woman has a mare with a foal; if someone guards the mare successfully for three days, the old woman will give him the choice of whichever horse he wishes. But if someone engages himself to watch the mare, and fails to guard her successfully for three days and three nights, he will lose his life."

On the next day the dragon went away, and the prince returned. The empress told him what the dragon had said. So the prince set off for the hill where the old woman was to be found.

When he entered her house, he said to her, "Good day, old woman!"

The old woman replied, "Bless you, my son! What brings you here?"

He replied, "I should like to take service with you."

The old woman said to him, "Very good, my son. I have a mare with a foal. If you watch her successfully for three days, I will give you one of these twelve horses of mine to take away, whichever you choose; but if you lose her, I shall take off your head."

Then she took him into the yard, where post after post was fixed in the ground, and on each was stuck a human head; only one remained vacant, and this cried out continually, "Old woman, give me a head!"

The old woman said to the prince, "Know that all these tried to watch the mare and the foal, but failed." But the prince wasn't frightened.

In the afternoon he mounted the mare and galloped uphill and downhill, and the foal galloped after. But at midnight, willy-nilly, tiredness crept over him, and he fell asleep. When he woke up at dawn, he still held the halter in his hand, but his arms were round a stump instead of the mare.

When he perceived this, the poor fellow became dizzy from terror, and started off to look for the mare. While he was looking for her, he came to an expanse of water, and, remembering the little fish, unfolded the handkerchief, took out the scale, and rubbed it between his fingers.

Up sprang the little fish out of the water, and lay before him. "What is the matter, adopted brother?" said the fish.

He replied, "The old woman's mare has escaped from me, and I don't know where she is."

The fish said to him, "She is among us; she has transformed herself into a fish, and her foal into a little fish. Flap the halter on the water, and call out, 'Coop! Coop! Old woman's mare!'"

The prince flapped the water with the halter, and called out, "Coop! Coop! Old woman's mare!" and immediately she transformed herself again into a mare, and – pop! – there she was at the edge of the water before him! He put the halter on her and mounted her, and trot, trot, they returned to the old woman's.

When he brought the mare in, the old woman gave him his dinner, but led the mare into the stable and scolded her, saying, "Among the fish, eh? You good-for-nothing rogue!"

The mare replied, "I was among the fish, but they told on me, because they are his friends."

The old woman advised her, "Go among the foxes."

The second day the prince mounted the mare, and galloped uphill and downhill, and the foal galloped after. When it was about midnight, drowsiness overcame him, and he fell asleep upon the mare's back. At dawn, when he awoke, he still held the halter in his hand, but his arms were round a stump. When he perceived this, he

set off again to seek her.

At once it came into his head what the old woman had said to the mare when she was leading it into the stable. Then he unwrapped the fox's hairs out of the handkerchief and rubbed them between his fingers. The fox immediately popped up before him.

"What is it, adopted brother?"

He replied, "The old woman's mare has run away."

The fox said to him, "She is among us; she has become a fox, and the foal a fox cub. Flap the ground with the halter, and call out, 'Coop! Coop! Old woman's mare!'"

The prince flapped and called, and the mare leaped out before him. Then he caught her and put the halter on her, mounted, and rode to the old woman's.

When he brought the mare home, the old woman gave him his dinner, led the mare off to the stable, and said, "Among the foxes, eh? You good-for-nothing rogue!"

The mare replied, "I was among them, but they are his friends, and told on me."

The old woman said to her, "Go among the crows."

The third day the prince again mounted the mare and galloped her uphill and downhill, and the foal galloped after. About midnight he became sleepy. When he awoke at dawn, he still held the halter in his hand, but his arms were round a stump.

As soon as he perceived this, he darted off again to seek the mare,

119

and as he was searching, it came into his head what the old woman had said the day before when scolding the mare. He took out the handkerchief and unwrapped the crow's feathers, rubbed them between his fingers, and – pop! – the crow was before him.

"What is it, adopted brother?"

The prince replied, "The old woman's mare has run away, and I don't know where she is."

The crow answered, "She is among us; she has become a crow, and the foal a young crow. Flap the halter in the air and cry, 'Coop! Coop! Old woman's mare!'"

The prince flapped the halter in the air and cried, "Coop! Coop! Old woman's mare!" and the mare transformed herself back from a crow into a mare, and came to him. Then he put the halter on her, mounted, and galloped off to the old woman's, the foal following behind.

The old woman gave him his dinner and led the mare into the stable, saying to her, "Among the crows, eh? You good-for-nothing rogue!"

The mare replied, "I was among them, but they are his friends, and told on me."

When the old woman came out, the prince said to her, "Well, old woman, I have served you honestly; now I ask you to give me what we agreed upon."

The old woman replied, "My son, what is agreed upon must be given. Here are twelve horses – choose whichever you please."

He replied, "I shan't pick and choose. Give me that scraggy one in the corner; that's the one I'd like."

The old woman tried to dissuade him. "Why choose that skinny one when there are so many good ones?"

But he flatly insisted, "Give me the one I ask for, that was our agreement."

The old woman twisted and turned, but she had to give him the one he asked for. Then he mounted the horse , and said "Farewell, old woman!"

"Goodbye, my son!"

Then he took the horse to a wood and groomed it, and it glittered like gold. Afterward, when he mounted the horse and gave it its head, it flew, flew like a bird, and in no time at all arrived at the dragon's palace.

As soon as he entered the courtyard, he told the empress to get ready for flight. She soon was ready; they both mounted the horse and set off.

They were not long gone when the dragon arrived home. He looked about. No empress. Then he said to his horse, "Shall we eat and drink, or shall we pursue?"

"Eat or not, drink or not, pursue or not, you won't catch him."

When the dragon heard this, he immediately mounted his horse, and started in pursuit. The prince and empress saw the dragon chasing them. They were terrified, and urged their horse to go quickly, but the horse answered them, "Never fear; there's no need to hurry."

The dragon chased them as fast as he could, and the horse he rode called to that which bore the prince and the empress, "Bless you, brother, wait! For I shall kill myself pursuing you."

The other replied, "Whose fault is it, if you're such a fool as to carry that monster on your back? Buck, and throw him to the ground, and then follow me."

When the dragon's horse heard this, he reared his head and bucked with his hindquarters, and bang went the dragon against a stone.

The dragon was smashed to pieces, and his horse followed the prince and empress. Then the empress caught and mounted it, and rode back with the prince to her own palace, where they reigned honorably as long as they lived.

A Good Deed Is Always Requited with Ill
Lithuania

A peasant walking in a forest found a dragon caught beneath a fallen tree. The dragon begged to be freed, and the man said, "What will you give me if I let you go?"

"I will reward you well," said the dragon, and the man set him free.

"Now for your reward," said the dragon. "You can be my lunch."

"You can't do that!" said the man. "I've done you a good deed."

But the dragon answered, "A good deed is always requited with ill."

The man begged for his life. He said, "Don't eat me yet. Let's walk along together, and ask the first three beings we meet to decide the matter."

The dragon agreed, and the pair went forward together until they met a dog. The peasant said, "Friend dog, decide between us."

"What's the matter?" asked the dog.

The man explained, "As I was walking along I came upon this dragon, who was imprisoned beneath a fallen tree. He said that if I freed him he would give me a rich reward. But now he wants to eat me! We have agreed that we shall ask the first three beings we meet to decide between us."

The dog replied, "When I was young, if a sow from a herd became threatening, and my master called upon me for aid, I used to spring forward and drive her back. But when I grew old and lost my teeth, my master forsook me. Now I'm left to fend for myself. The dragon is right. Good deeds are always requited with ill." And the dog added to the dragon, "Eat him!"

The pair went on, and met a horse, to whom the man said, "Dear horse, please decide between us."

"What's the argument?" asked the horse.

The peasant told the whole story, as he had told it to the dog.

The horse replied, "When I was in my prime, my master petted me. Now I am old and tired, he has cast me out. The dragon is right. A good deed is always requited with ill." Turning to the dragon, he said, "Eat the man!"

The pair went on again, and met a fox, to whom the man said, "Good fox, please judge between us."

The fox listened to the man's story, and then said, "What will you give me for deciding this case?"

"I will give you a goose," the man said.

"To make a wise decision," said the fox, "I need to see where all this happened. Take me to the spot." So the peasant and the dragon went back with the fox to the fallen tree.

"I can't really picture the scene in my mind's eye," said the fox. And he said to the man, "Just lift the tree up," and to the dragon, "Just lie down as you were." When the dragon lay down, the fox shouted to the man, "Let the tree drop!" The dragon was trapped again, and the fox told him, "You can stay as you were."

The man went home, and the fox went with him. The man left the fox outside the house, telling him that he would bring him the goose. He went inside, and told his wife everything that had happened, and described the fine behavior of the quick-witted fox. "I'll just take him that goose I promised him," he said.

"You fool," said the wife. "Why waste a goose? Take your gun and shoot the creature dead. You will be able to sell the skin!"

The man took the goose in one hand and his gun in the other, behind his back. He went up to the fox and, when he was near enough, shot him.

As the fox lay dying, he gasped with his last breath, "A good deed is always requited with ill."

124

Prince Unexpected

Poland

There was a king and queen who had been married for three years, but had no children, at which they were both much distressed.

Once upon a time the king found himself obliged to make a visit of inspection round his dominions; he took leave of his queen, set off, and was not home for eight months. Toward the end of the ninth month the king returned from his progress through his country, and was already hard by his capital city, when, as he journeyed over an uninhabited plain during the most scorching heat of summer, he felt such a great thirst that he sent his servants round about to see if they could find water anywhere and let him know of it at once. The servants dispersed in various directions, sought in vain for a whole hour, and returned without success to the king.

The thirst-tormented king proceeded to traverse the whole plain far and wide himself, not believing that there was not a spring somewhere or other; on he rode, and at a level spot, on which there had not previously been any water, he saw a well with a new wooden fence round it, full to the brim with spring water, in the midst of which floated a silver cup with a golden handle.

The king sprang from his horse and reached for the cup with his right hand; but the cup, just as if it were alive and had eyes, darted quickly to one side. The king knelt down and began to try to catch it, now with his right hand, now with his left, but it moved and dodged away in such a manner that, not being able to seize it with one hand, he tried to catch it with both. But scarcely had he reached out with both hands when the cup dived like a fish, and floated again on the surface.

"Hang it!" thought the king. "I can't help myself with the cup, I'll manage without it." He then bent down to the water, which was as clear as crystal and as cold as ice, and began in his thirst to drink.

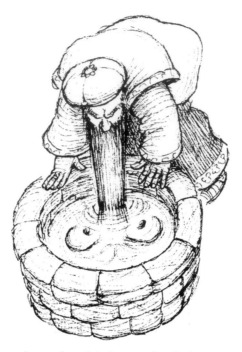

Meanwhile his long beard, which reached down to his belt, dipped into the water. When he had quenched his thirst, he wanted to get up again, but something was holding his beard and wouldn't let it go. He pulled once, and again, but it was no use; he cried out in anger, "Who's there? Let go!"

"It's I, the king of the underworld, immortal Bony, and I shall not let go till you give me that which you left unknowingly at home, and which you do not expect to find on your return." The king looked into the depth of the well, and there was a huge head like a tub, with green eyes and a mouth from ear to ear, and the creature was holding the king by the beard with extended claws like those of a crab, and laughing mischievously.

The king thought that a thing of which he had not known before starting, and which he did not expect on his return, could not be of great value, so he said to the apparition, "I give it." Immortal Bony burst into laughter and vanished with a flash of fire, and with him vanished also the well, the water, the wooden fence, and the cup; and the king was again on a hillock by a little wood kneeling on dry sand, and there was nothing more. The king got up, crossed himself, sprang onto his horse, hastened to his attendants, and rode on.

126

In a week or maybe a fortnight the king arrived at his capital; the people came out in crowds to meet him; he went in procession to the great court of the palace and entered the corridor. In the corridor stood the queen awaiting him, and holding close to her bosom a cushion, on which lay a child, beautiful as the moon, kicking in swaddling clothes. Then the king understood, and, sighing painfully, said to himself, "This is what I left without knowing and have found without expecting!" And bitterly, bitterly did he weep. All marveled, but nobody dared to ask the cause. The king took his son in his arms without saying a word and gazed long on his innocent face. He carried the baby into the palace himself, laid him in the cradle, and, suppressing his sorrow, devoted himself to the government of his realm. But he was never his old cheerful self again, since he was perpetually tormented by the thought that some day Bony would claim his son.

Meanwhile weeks, months, and years flowed on, and no one came for his son. The prince, named Unexpected, grew and developed, and eventually became a handsome youth. The king in course of time began to forget what had taken place, but alas! Everybody did not forget so easily.

Once the prince, while hunting in a forest, became separated from his suite and found himself in a savage wilderness. Suddenly there appeared before him a hideous old man with green eyes, who said, "How do you do, Prince Unexpected? You have made me wait for you a long time."

"Who are you?"

"That you will find out hereafter, but now, when you return to your father, greet him from me, and tell him that I should be glad if he would close accounts with me, for if he doesn't soon get out of my debt, he will repent it bitterly." After saying this the hideous old man disappeared, and the prince in amazement turned his horse, rode home, and told the king his adventure. The king turned as pale as a sheet, and revealed the frightful secret to his son.

"Don't cry, Father!" replied the prince. "It isn't a great misfortune! I shall manage to force Bony to renounce the right over me, which he tricked you out of in so underhand a manner. But if I do not return within a year, then we shall see each other no more." The prince prepared for his journey, the king gave him a suit of steel

127

armor, a sword, and a horse, and the queen hung round his neck a
cross of pure gold. At leave-taking they embraced affectionately,
wept heartily, and the prince rode off.

On he rode one day, two days, three days, and at the end of the
fourth day at the setting of the sun he came to the shore of the sea.
In the bay he saw twelve dresses, white as snow, though in the
water, as far as the eye could reach, there was no living soul to be
seen; only twelve white geese were swimming at a distance from
the shore. Curious to know to whom the dresses belonged, he took
one of them, let his horse loose in a meadow, concealed himself in a
neighboring thicket, and waited to see what would come to pass.
Thereupon the geese, after disporting themselves in the sea, swam
to the shore; eleven of them went to the dresses; each threw herself
on the ground and became a beautiful girl, dressed herself with
speed, and flew away into the plain.

The twelfth goose, the last and prettiest of all, did not venture to
come out on the shore, but only wistfully stretched out her neck,
looking on all sides. On seeing the prince she called out with a

human voice, "Prince Unexpected, give me my dress; I will be grateful to you in return." The prince hearkened to her; he placed the dress on the grass, and modestly turned away in another direction.

The goose came out on the grass, changed herself into a girl, dressed herself hastily, and stood before the prince; she was young and more beautiful than eye had seen or ear heard of. Blushing, she gave him her white hand, and, casting her eyes down, said with a pleasing voice, "I thank you, good prince, for hearkening to me. I am the youngest daughter of immortal Bony; he has twelve young daughters, and rules beneath the earth. My father, prince, has long been waiting for you and is very angry; however, don't grieve, and don't be frightened, but do as I tell you. As soon as you see King Bony, fall at once on your knees, and, paying no regard to his outcry, upbraiding, and threats, approach him boldly. What will happen afterward you will learn, but now we must part." On saying this the princess stamped on the ground with her little foot; the ground sprang open at once, and they descended through the earth, right into Bony's palace, which though underground shone brighter than our sun.

The prince stepped boldly into the reception room. Bony was sitting on a golden throne with a glittering crown on his head; his eyes gleamed like two saucers of green glass and his hands were like the nippers of a crab. As soon as he saw Bony at a distance, the prince fell on his knees, and Bony yelled so horribly that the vaults of his underground realm quaked; but the prince boldly moved on his knees toward the throne, and, when he was only a few paces from it, the king smiled and said, "You are lucky; you have succeeded in making me smile. Therefore you may remain in our realm, but before you become a true citizen you must fulfill three commands of mine. It is late today, we will begin tomorrow; meanwhile go to your room."

The prince slept comfortably in the room assigned to him, and early on the morrow Bony summoned him and said, "We will see, prince, what you can do. In the course of the following night build me a palace of pure marble; let the windows be of crystal and the roof of gold, with an elegant garden round about it, and in the garden seats and fountains; if you build it, you will gain my love; if not, I shall command that your head be cut off."

The prince, hearing this, returned to his apartment, and was sitting mournfully thinking of the death that threatened him, when outside at the window a bee came buzzing and said, "Let me in!" He opened the lattice, in flew the bee, and the princess, Bony's youngest daughter, appeared before the wondering prince. "What are you thinking about, Prince Unexpected?"

"Alas! I am thinking that your father wishes to deprive me of life."

"Don't be afraid! Lie down to sleep, and when you get up tomorrow morning your palace will be ready."

So, too, it came to pass. At dawn the prince came out of his room and saw a more beautiful palace than he had ever seen, and Bony, when he saw it, wondered, and wouldn't believe his own eyes. "Well! You have won this time, and now you must fulfill my second command. I shall place my twelve daughters before you tomorrow; if you do not guess which of them is the youngest, you will place your head beneath the axe."

"I, unable to recognize the youngest princess!" said the prince in his room. "What difficulty can there be in that?"

"This," answered the princess, flying into the room in the shape of a bee, "that if I don't help you, you won't recognize me, for we are all so alike that even our father only distinguishes us by our dress."

"What am I to do?"

"What, indeed! The youngest will be the one over whose right eye you see a ladybug. Just keep your eyes open. Good luck!"

In the morning King Bony again summoned Prince Unexpected. The princesses stood in a row side by side, all dressed alike and with eyes cast down. The prince looked and marveled how alike all the princesses were; he went past them once, twice – he did not find the appointed token; but the third time he saw a ladybug over the eyebrow of one, and cried out, "This is the youngest princess!"

"How the deuce have you guessed it?" said Bony angrily. "There must be some trickery here. I must deal with your lordship differently. In three hours you will come here again, and will show your cleverness in my presence. I shall light a straw, and you will stitch a pair of boots before it goes out, and if you don't do it, you will perish."

The prince returned despondent and found the bee already in his apartment. "Why sad again, prince?"

"How shouldn't I be sad, when your father wants me to stitch him a pair of boots, for what sort of cobbler am I?"

"What will you do?"

"What am I to do? I can't stitch the boots, but I'm not afraid of death: one can die but once!"

"No, prince, you shall not die! I will try to rescue you, and we will either escape together or perish together! We must flee. There's nothing else to be done." Saying this, the princess spat on one of the windowpanes, and the spittle immediately froze. She then went out of the room with the prince, locked the door after her, and threw the key far away; then, taking each other by the hand, they ascended rapidly, and in a moment found themselves on the very spot from which they had descended into the underground realm; there was the selfsame sea, the selfsame shore overgrown with rushes and thornbushes, the selfsame fresh meadow, and in the meadow cantered the prince's well-fed horse, who, as soon as he saw his rider, came galloping straight to him. The prince didn't stop long to think, but sprang on his horse, the princess seated herself behind him, and off they set as swift as an arrow.

King Bony at the appointed hour did not wait for Prince Unexpected, but sent to ask him why he did not appear. Finding the door locked, the servants knocked at it vigorously, and the spittle answered them from the middle of the room in the prince's voice, "I'm coming!" The servants carried this answer to the king; he waited, waited, but no prince came; he therefore again sent the same servants, who heard the same answer: "I'm coming!" and carried what they had heard to the king.

"What's this? Does he mean to make fun of me?" shouted the king in wrath. "Go at once, break the door open, and bring him to me!" The servants hurried off, broke open the door, and rushed in. What, indeed? There was nobody there, and the spittle on the pane of glass was splitting with laughter at them. Bony almost burst with rage, and ordered them all to start off in pursuit of the prince, threatening them with death if they returned emptyhanded. They sprang on horseback and hastened away after the prince and princess.

Meanwhile Prince Unexpected and the princess, Bony's daughter, were hurrying away on their spirited horse, and during their rapid flight heard "Tramp, tramp," behind them. The prince sprang from the horse, put his ear to the ground, and said, "They are pursuing us."

"Then," said the princess, "we have no time to lose." Instantly she transformed herself into a river, changed the prince into a bridge, the horse into a raven, and made the grand highway beyond the bridge divide into three roads. Swiftly on the fresh track hastened the pursuers, but when they came to the bridge, they stood stupefied. They saw the track up to the bridge, but beyond it disappeared, and the highway divided into three roads. There was nothing to be done but to return, emptyhanded.

Bony shouted with rage, and cried out, "A bridge and a river! It was they. How was it that you did not guess it? Back, and don't return without them!" The pursuers recommenced the pursuit.

"I hear 'Tramp, tramp!'" whispered the princess, Bony's daughter, in fear to Prince Unexpected, who sprang from the saddle, put his ear to the ground, and replied, "They are making haste, and are not far off." That instant the princess and prince, and with them also their horse, became a gloomy forest, in which were roads, byroads, and footpaths without number, and on one of them it seemed that two riders were hastening on a horse. Following the fresh track, the pursuers came up to the forest, and when they spotted the fugitives in it, they hastened quickly after them. On and on hurried the pursuers, seeing continually before them a thick forest, a wide road and the fugitives on it; now, now they thought to overtake them, when the fugitives and the thick forest suddenly vanished, and they found themselves at the selfsame place from which they had started in pursuit. So they returned once more emptyhanded to immortal Bony.

"A horse, a horse! I'll go myself! They won't escape out of my hands!" yelled Bony, foaming at the mouth. He started in pursuit.

Again the princess said to Prince Unexpected, "I think they are pursuing us, and this time it is Bony, my father himself. But the first church is the boundary of his dominion, and he won't be able to pursue us farther. Give me your golden cross." The prince took off his loving mother's gift and gave it to the princess, and in a moment she was transformed into a church, he into the priest, and the horse into the bell; and at that instant up came Bony.

"Monk!" Bony said to the priest. "Have you not seen some travelers on horseback?"

"Only just now Prince Unexpected rode this way with the princess, Bony's daughter. They came into the church, performed their devotions, gave money for a mass for your good health, and ordered me to present their respects to you if you should ride this way." Bony, too, returned emptyhanded. But Prince Unexpected rode on with the princess, Bony's daughter, in no further fear of pursuit.

They rode gently on, till they saw before them a beautiful town; the prince felt an irresistible longing to go there. "Prince," said the princess, "don't go; my heart fears misfortune there."

"I'll only ride there for a short time, and look round the town, and we'll then proceed on our journey."

"It's easy enough to ride there, but will it be as easy to return? Nevertheless, as you absolutely desire it, go, and I will remain here in the form of a white stone till you return. Be careful, my beloved; the king, the queen, and the princess, their daughter, will come out to meet you, and with them will be a beautiful little boy. Don't kiss him, for, if you do, you will forget me at once, and will never set eyes on me more in the world; I shall die of despair. I will wait for you here on the road for three days, and if on the third day you don't return, remember that I perish, and perish all through you." The prince took leave and rode to the town, and the princess transformed herself into a white stone, and remained on the road.

One day passed, a second passed, a third also passed, and nothing was seen of the prince. Poor princess! He had not obeyed her counsel; in the town, the king, the queen, and the princess their daughter, had come out to meet him, and with them walked a little boy, a curly-headed chatterbox, with eyes as bright as stars. The child rushed straight into the arms of the prince, who was so captivated by the beauty of the lad that he forgot everything, and kissed the child affectionately. That moment his memory darkened, and he utterly forgot the princess, Bony's daughter.

The princess lay as a white stone by the wayside, one day, two days, and when the third day passed and the prince did not return from the town, she transformed herself into a cornflower and sprang in among the rye by the roadside. "Here I shall stay by the roadside; maybe some passerby will pull me up or trample me into the ground," said she, and tears like dewdrops glittered on the azure petals. Just then an old man came along the road, saw the cornflower in the rye by the wayside, and was captivated by its beauty. He pulled it carefully from the ground, carried it into his dwelling, set it in a flowerpot, watered it, and began to tend it lovingly. But – O marvel! – from the moment that the cornflower was brought into his dwelling, all kind of wonders began to happen there. Scarcely was the old man awake, when everything in the house was already set in order; nowhere was the least atom of dust remaining. At noon when he came home, dinner was all ready, the table set; he had but to sit down and eat as much as he wanted. The old man wondered and wondered, till at last terror took possession of him, and he went for advice to an old witch of his acquaintance in the neighborhood. "Do this," the witch advised him. "Get up before the first morning light, before the cocks crow to announce dawn, and watch out for what begins to stir first in the house, and whatever stirs, cover it with this napkin: what will happen then, you will see."

The old man didn't close his eyes the whole night, and as soon as the first gleam appeared and things began to be visible in the house, he saw how the cornflower suddenly moved in the flowerpot, sprang out, and began to stir about the room; when simultaneously everything began to put itself in its place; the dust began to sweep itself clean away, and the fire kindled itself in the stove. The old man sprang cleverly out of his bed and placed the cloth on the flower as it endeavored to escape, and lo! The flower became a beautiful girl: the princess, Bony's daughter.

"What have you done?" cried the princess. "Why have you brought life back to me again? My betrothed, Prince Unexpected, has forgotten me, and therefore I do not want to live."

"Your betrothed, Prince Unexpected, is going to be married today; the wedding feast is ready, and the guests are beginning to assemble."

The princess wept, but after a while dried her tears, dressed herself like a village girl, and went into the town. She came to the royal kitchen, where there was great noise and bustle. She went up to the clerk of the kitchen with humble and attractive grace, and said in a sweet voice, "Dear sir, do me one favor; allow me to make a wedding cake for Prince Unexpected."

As he was very busy, the first impulse of the clerk of the kitchen was to give the girl a rebuff, but when he looked at her, the words died on his lips, and he answered kindly, "Ah, my beauty of beauties! Do what you will; I will hand the prince your cake myself."

The cake was soon baked, and all the invited guests were sitting at table. The clerk of the kitchen himself placed a huge cake on a silver dish before the prince; but scarce had the prince made a cut in the side of it, when lo! An unheard-of marvel displayed itself in the presence of all. A gray tom-pigeon and a white hen-pigeon came out of the cake; the tom-pigeon danced along the table, and the hen-pigeon danced after him, cooing:

> "Stay, stay, my pigeon-love, oh stay!
> Don't from your true love flee away;
> Don't leave me here alone like this;
> The prince betrayed his true love with a kiss."

Scarcely had Prince Unexpected heard this cooing of the pigeon, when he regained his lost memory, rose from the table, and rushed to the door. Behind the door the princess, Bony's daughter, took him by the hand; they went together down the corridor, and before them stood their horse saddled and bridled.

Why delay? Prince Unexpected and the princess, Bony's daughter, sprang on the horse, started on the road, and at last arrived happily in the realm of Prince Unexpected's father. The king and queen received them with joy and merriment, and didn't wait long before they prepared them a magnificent wedding, the like of which eye never saw and ear never heard of.

The Cottage in the Sky

Byelorussia

An old man and an old woman sat together and ate some green peas; but one of the peas fell under the floor and sprouted. It grew until it reached the floor, and when the man and the woman broke a floorboard it continued until it reached the ceiling. The man and the woman made a hole in the ceiling for it, and again in the roof. The pea continued to grow into the sky, and it produced pods with peas in them.

"Look, old man," said the old woman to her husband. "Our little pea has already reached a great height. God knows how far it has gone, but neither you nor I know. I wish I could find out."

"Well," replied the man. "If you want to make the attempt, do so. You are more agile than I am; climb up, and perhaps you will learn."

The old woman climbed up the pea, and though it was hard she kept at it till she reached the top. There, she found a small hut standing on the very summit. She went in, and found nobody at home.

The hut was not built like our cottages. The walls were made of pie, the stove was pancake, the tables were cheese, the benches were gingerbread, and there was plenty of everything, including butter, curds, and honey, all of the best.

The old woman ate whatever she liked, and continued to eat till at last she could eat no more. Then she crawled under the stove and hid herself lest anyone should come. Rolled up like a ball, she held her breath and lay in a corner.

Three goats, who were sisters, entered the hut. One of them had two eyes and two ears, another had three eyes and three ears, while the last had four eyes and four ears. The goats came into the hut, sniffed the air, and got scent of a Russian. They said among themselves, "There is a stranger in the hut. There is a smell like a Russian's. Let us search everywhere!" They searched thoroughly, looking in all the corners and crannies, without finding the old woman. Then they said, "There is nothing to be done. There can't be anyone here now, but we must guard against anyone coming later. We will eat a little," they said, "and then two of us will go into the field, while the third remains at home on watch."

The goats ate whatever they fancied. One ate honey, one ate cracknels, and the third ate gingerbread. Then two of them went out to the field, and left at home the goat which had two eyes. Before leaving, the sisters said to her, "Look, sister, look through both eyes, so that no harm shall befall us."

"Certainly!" replied the goat with two eyes. "You go, and I will stand watch."

The old woman heard this conversation, and wondered how she could keep the goat from finding her out. At last she sang a quiet song: "Eye sleep, second eye sleep; ear shut, second ear shut!" And as she sang, first one of the goat's eyes closed and then the other eye; next one ear and then the other ear. When the goat was asleep, the old woman crawled out from under the stove, ate up a great deal, and concealed herself as before.

The two goats came in from the field and saw that their sister was fast asleep. "Sister, oh, sister!" they called. "Wake up! Why have you fallen asleep?" They could scarcely wake her.

"Ah!" said the sister with two ears. "I really was fast asleep. But what does it matter? No harm has come to the cottage. All has been still and peaceful."

"That may be," said the others, "but nevertheless there is a Russian smell here. Next time we must keep a better watch."

The sisters ate what they wished, two of them went out to the field, and the sister with three eyes and three ears stayed behind.

The old woman was lying under the stove and, feeling peckish once more, sang quietly, "Eye sleep, second eye sleep, third eye sleep; ear shut, second ear shut, third ear shut!" The goat's eyes and ears closed, and the old woman crawled out, ate various kinds of food, and again hid under the stove.

When the goats returned from the field, they saw their sister asleep, and smelt the Russian smell again. "As this has happened," they said, "it will be safer next time to leave behind the sister with four eyes and four ears!" They roused the three-eyed sister and

asked her, "Did you see or hear anything?"

"I saw and heard nothing," was the reply. "I was fast asleep; a great drowsiness fell upon me."

The goats ate whatever they fancied, and two of them went for a walk in the field, leaving at home the sister who had four eyes and four ears.

The old woman, lying beneath the stove, grew hungry again for the good things of the hut, and so she sang, "Eye sleep, second eye sleep, third eye sleep; ear shut, second ear shut, third ear shut!" But she forgot the existence of the fourth eye and the fourth ear, and the goat, though three of her eyes and three of her ears were closed, could see with the fourth eye and hear with the fourth ear.

As soon as the old woman crawled out, the goat woke and said, "Ah! It is you that has come into our little cottage and eaten our gingerbread and other good things! Where have you come from?"

"I do not belong up here," replied the old woman. "Out of curiosity I have roamed from earth up to the sky."

"But how did you manage to get here?"

"I climbed up the green pea, which grows through our cottage."

"Well," said the goat, "I will not do you any harm. When my

sisters come home, we will decide your fate."

Then the sisters returned and saw the old woman. "Ah," they said, "so it is you who has been visiting our home and gobbling up our food when we were away! Who are you?"

"I managed to get here by climbing up a green pea from earth; I was curious about you."

"Well," said the goats, "we will not do anything to you now. But you must go at once, and never come back!"

The old woman promised to obey the goats' command, and they supplied her with a small bag containing a variety of sweetmeats, gingerbread, nuts, cheese, cracknels, and indeed a little of everything in the cottage, and then they sent her on her way.

The old woman climbed down the pea and reached her home. "Old man!" she said. "Tell me where I have been!"

"Where indeed?" asked her husband.

"I have been up to the top of the pea," she told him, "and climbed all the way down again."

"Is it possible?"

"It is true! And I have seen such wonderful things and eaten such delicacies!" She told the old man all about the little hut at the top of the green pea. "I would go back this minute," she said, "but the goats forbade me to return."

"Let us go up together," said the old man. "They will not hurt two of us. I ought to see this!"

"Very well," said his wife, and they started to climb the pea, and all their family with them.

First of all the old man climbed, with a hatchet at his waist. The old woman went next, and their granddaughter followed her. They climbed and climbed a long way, when suddenly the old man coughed down in the direction of the old woman, and she coughed down to her granddaughter, and so on all the way down. The green pea shook with all their coughing, and fell, and they were all killed.

So they never reached the cottage in the sky. No one knows where they fell; when they perished they left no trace. Since their time, nobody has found the cottage in the sky again, and no one has learnt any more about it.

The Wizard

Ukraine

There was once in our village here a certain Avstriyat, who was such a wizard that he could control the weather.

It happened that we were cutting corn in the country, when a cloud came up. We began to hurry with the sheaves, but he took no notice. He cut and cut away by himself, and smoked his pipe, and said, "Don't be frightened. There'll be no rain."

Lo and behold, there was no rain.

Once – all this I saw with my own eyes – we were cutting rye, when the sky became black and the wind rose; it began to whistle, at first far off, but then right over our heads. There was thunder, lightning, whirlwind: such a tempest that we could only put up our hands and say, "O God! Thy will be done!" But Avstriyat said, "Don't be frightened. There'll be no rain." He just smoked his pipe out, and cut away quietly by himself.

Soon, up came a man on a black horse, and all black himself; he darted straight up to Avstriyat. "Hey! Give permission!" he said.

"No, I won't," said Avstriyat.

"Give permission; be merciful."

"I won't. It would make it impossible to harvest the rye."

The black horseman bowed to the man, and sped off across the countryside.

Then the black cloud became gray, and whitened. Our elders feared that there would be hail. But Avstriyat took no notice. He cut the corn by himself, and smoked his pipe. But again a horseman came up; he sped over the country still quicker than the first. But this one was all in white, on a white horse.

"Give permission!" he shouted to Avstriyat.

"I won't."

"Give permission, for God's sake!"

"I won't. It would be impossible to get such a quantity in."

142

"Please! Give permission; I can't hold out!"

Then, and not till then, did Avstriyat relent. "Well, then, you can let it go, but only into that valley beyond the plain."

Scarcely had he spoken, when the horseman disappeared, and hail poured down in basketfuls into the valley. In a short hour it filled the valley to the brim.

Fate

Serbia

There were two brothers living together in a house, one of whom did all the work, while the other did nothing but laze around, eating and drinking whatever came to hand. And God gave them prosperity in everything – in cattle, in horses, in sheep, in swine, in bees, and in everything else.

One day, the hard worker thought to himself, "Why should I work for that lazybones as well? It is better that we should part. Then I would be working only for myself, and he could do as he liked."

So he said to his brother, "Brother, it isn't right. I do all the work, and you're no help at all. You just eat and drink what I provide. I have made up my mind that we should part."

The lazybones tried to dissuade him. "Don't, brother; it is good for us to live together. You have charge of everything, both yours and mine, and I am content whatever you do."

But the hard worker had made up his mind, so his brother gave way, and told him, "If it must be, it must be: You go your way, and I'll go mine. You divide our possessions; you know what's what."

Then they divided everything between them, and went their separate ways.

The do-nothing engaged a herdsman for his cattle, a stable lad for his horses, a shepherd for his sheep, a goatherd for his goats, a swineherd for his swine, a beekeeper for his bees. He told them, "I leave all my property in your hands and God's," and began to live just as he had before.

His brother still did all the work about his property himself, watching and worrying, but for all his hard work he saw no prosperity, only loss. From day to day things went from bad to worse, till he was so poor that he had no shoes, but went barefoot. Then he said to himself, "I will go to my brother, and see how he has fared." He did so, and on the way came to a flock of sheep in a meadow. There was no shepherd in sight, but a very beautiful girl was sitting there, spinning golden thread. He bid her good day and asked her whose the sheep were.

She replied, "The sheep belong to the person to whom I belong."

He asked her further, "To whom do you belong?"

She answered, "I am your brother's luck."

He was put out, and said to her, "And where is *my* luck?"

The girl answered him, "Your luck is far from you."

"But can I find it?" he asked, and she replied, "You can. Go, seek for it."

When he heard this, and saw that his brother's sheep were good – so good that they couldn't be better – he went straight off to his brother.

When his brother saw him, he pitied him, and began to weep. "Why have you waited so long?" he asked. Then, seeing him bareheaded and barefoot, he gave him at once a pair of boots and some money.

Afterwards, when they had enjoyed each other's company for some days, the visitor rose up to go to his own house. When he got home, he put a knapsack on his back with some bread in it, took a staff in his hand, and went into the world to look for his luck. As he traveled, he came to a large wood. There he saw a gray-haired old woman asleep under a bush, and he reached out his staff to give her a nudge.

She barely raised herself up, and, hardly opening her eyes for the rheum, told him, "You should thank God that I fell asleep, for if I had been awake, you wouldn't have obtained even that pair of boots."

Then he said to her, "Who are you, that I shouldn't even have obtained this pair of boots?"

She replied, "I am your luck."

When he heard this, he began to beat his breast. "If you are my luck, good riddance to you! Who gave you to me?"

She answered, "Fate gave me to you."

"And where is this Fate?" he asked.

She answered, "Go and look for him." And with that, she disappeared.

The man went to look for Fate. As he journeyed, he came to a village, and saw in the village a large farmhouse, with a fire burning in the hearth. Saying to himself, "This looks like some merry making or festival," he went in. On the fire was a large cauldron, in which supper was cooking, and in front of the fire sat the master of the house. "Good evening!" said the traveler.

The master replied, "Sit down, with my blessing." Then the farmer asked him where he came from, and where he was going.

The traveler told him everything: how he had been a master, how he had become impoverished, and how he was now going to Fate to ask him why he was so poor.

Then he asked of the farmer why he was preparing such a lot of food, and the farmer said, "Well, my brother, I am master here, and have enough of everything, but no matter how much I cook, it is never enough for my servants. They eat as if a dragon were in their stomachs. When we begin to eat, you'll see what happens."

When they sat down to eat, everybody snatched and grabbed from everybody else, and that large cauldron of food was empty in no time. After supper, a maidservant came in, put all the bones in a heap, and threw them behind the stove. The traveler began to wonder why the young woman threw the bones behind the stove, till all at once out came two old poverty-stricken specters, as dry as ghosts, and began to suck the bones.

Then he asked the master of the house, "What's this, brother, behind the stove?"

He replied, "Those, brother, are my father and mother; they are fettered to this world, they will not quit it."

The next day, at his departure, the master of the house said to him, "Brother, remember me, too, if you do find Fate, and ask him what manner of misfortune it is that my servants are so hungry, and why my father and mother do not die."

The traveler promised to ask Fate the question, took leave of the farmer, and went on to look for Fate. After a long time he came to another village, and begged at one house that they would take him in for a night's lodging. They did so, and asked him where he was going; and he told them all in order, what it was, and how it was.

Then they said to him, "In God's name, brother, when you get there, ask him about us too, why our cows give no milk."

He promised them to ask Fate the question, and the next day went on. As he went, he came to a stream of water, and began to shout, "Stream! Stream! Carry me across."

The stream asked him, "Where are you going?"

He told it where he was going. Then the stream carried him across, and said to him, "I pray you, brother, ask Fate why I have no tributaries."

He promised the stream to ask the question, and then went on. He went on for a long time, and at last came to a wood, where he found a hermit, whom he asked about Fate. The hermit answered, "Go over that hill, and you will come to his house. When you come into Fate's presence, do not say a word, but do exactly what he does, until he questions you himself."

The man thanked the hermit, and went over the hill. When he came to Fate's house, that was a sight to see! It was like an emperor's palace; there were menservants and maidservants there; everything was in good order, and Fate himself was sitting at a golden dinner table having supper. When the man saw this, he, too, sat down at the table and began to eat.

After supper, Fate lay down to sleep, and the man lay down too. About midnight a terrible noise arose, and out of the noise a voice was heard calling, "Fate! Fate! So many souls have been born today;

assign them what you will.''

Then Fate arose, and opened a chest with money in it, and began to throw gold coins behind him, saying, ''As with me today, so with them for life!''

When the next day dawned, that great palace was gone. Instead there was a large house; and in it again there was enough of everything.

At the approach of evening Fate sat down to supper, and the traveler sat down with him; but neither spoke a single word. After supper they lay down to sleep. About midnight a terrible noise began, and out of the noise was heard a voice calling, ''Fate! Fate! so many souls have been born today; assign them what you will.''

Then Fate arose, and opened the money chest; it was full of silver coins, with an occasional gold one. Fate began to scatter the coins behind him, saying, "As with me today, so with them for life."

When the next day dawned, that house was gone. In its place there stood a smaller one.

The same happened every night. Every morning Fate's house became smaller till finally nothing remained of it but a poky cottage.

Fate took a spade, and began to dig; the man, too, took a spade and began to dig, and thus they dug all day. When it was evening, Fate took a piece of bread, broke off half of it, and gave it to him. That was their supper, and afterwards they lay down to sleep. About midnight, as usual a terrible noise began, and out of the noise was heard a voice calling, "Fate! Fate! So many souls have been born today; assign them what you will."

Then Fate arose, opened the chest, and began to scatter behind him nothing but bits of rag, and here and there a day laborer's wage-penny, shouting, "As with me today, so with them for life."

When he arose on the next day, the cottage was transformed once more into a large palace, like the one that had been there on the first day.

Then Fate asked the traveler, "Why have you come?"

The man told Fate all his troubles and said that he had come to ask him why he gave him evil luck.

Fate then said to him, "You saw how the first night I scattered gold coins and what took place afterward. As it was with me the night when anyone was born, so will it be with him for life. You were born on an unlucky night, so you will be poor for life; your brother was born on a lucky night, and he will be lucky for life. But, as you have been so resolute, and have taken so much trouble, I will tell you how you may help yourself. Your brother has a daughter, Militza, who is lucky, just as her father is; adopt her, and whatever you acquire, say that it is all hers."

Then the traveler thanked Fate, and said to him, "In a village there is a wealthy peasant, who has enough of everything; but he is unlucky in this, that his servants can never be satisfied: they eat up a cauldron full of food at a single meal, and even that is too little for them. And this peasant's father and mother are, as it were, fettered to this world; they are old and discolored, and dried up like ghosts, but cannot die. He begged me, Fate, to ask you why that was the case."

Then Fate replied, "All that is because he does not honor his father and mother, throwing their food behind the stove. If he put them in the best place at table, and if he gave them the first cup of brandy, and the first cup of wine, his servants would not eat half so much, and his parents' souls would be set at liberty."

After this the man again questioned Fate. "In a village, where I spent the night in a house, the householder complained to me that his cows gave no milk, and he begged me to ask why this was the case."

Fate replied, "That is because on his saint's day he slaughters the worst animals. If he slaughtered the best he had, his cows would all give milk."

Then the traveler asked Fate about the stream of water. "Why does that stream of water have no tributaries?"

Fate replied, "Because it has never drowned a human being. But don't tell it till it has carried you across, for if you tell it, it will immediately drown you."

Then he thanked Fate, and went home.

When he came to the stream, it asked him, "What is the news from Fate?"

He replied, "Carry me over, and then I will tell you." When the stream had carried him over, he ran on a little, and, when he had got far enough away, he turned and shouted to the stream, "Stream! Stream! You have never drowned a human being, therefore you have no tributaries."

When the stream heard that, it overflowed its banks, and made after him; but the man outran it.

Then he came to the man whose cattle gave no milk. The householder was impatiently waiting for him. "What news, brother, in God's name? Have you asked Fate the question?"

He replied, "I have; and Fate says, when you celebrate your saint's day, you slaughter the worst animals; but if you slaughter the best you have, all your cows will give milk."

When the householder heard this, he said, "Stay with me, brother. It isn't three days to my name-day, and if what you say is really true, I will make it worth your while."

The man stayed till the name-day. Then the householder slaughtered his best ox, and from that time forth his cows gave milk.

After this, the householder gave the traveler five head of cattle. The man thanked him and proceeded on his way.

When he came to the village of the farmer who had the insatiable servants, the farmer was impatiently expecting him. "How is it, brother, in God's name? What says Fate?"

The man replied, "Fate says you do not honor your father and mother, but throw their food behind the stove for them to eat; if you put them in the best place at table, and give them the first cup of brandy and the first cup of wine, your people will not eat half as much, and your father and mother will be content."

When the farmer heard this, he told his wife, and she immediately washed and combed her father- and mother-in-law, and put nice shoes on their feet; and, when evening came, the farmer put them in the best place at table, and gave them the first cup of brandy and the first cup of wine.

From that time forth the household could not eat half what they did before, and on the next day both the father and the mother departed this life.

Then the farmer gave the traveler two oxen; he thanked him, and went home.

When he came to his own village, his neighbors began to congratulate him and ask him, "Whose are these cattle?"

He replied to everybody, "Brother, they are my niece Militza's."

When he got home he immediately went off to his brother, and began to beg him, "Brother, give me your daughter Militza to be my daughter. For I have no one."

His brother replied, "It is good, brother; Militza is yours."

He took Militza home, and afterward prospered, because he always said that everything was Militza's.

Once he went out into the field to tend some rye. The rye was beautiful; it could not be better. Just then a stranger happened to come up, and asked him, "Whose is this rye?"

He forgot himself, and said, "Mine."

The moment he said that, the rye caught fire and began to burn. When he saw this, he ran after the man crying, "Stop, brother! It is not mine; it belongs to Militza, my niece."

Then the fire in the rye went out, and the man remained lucky with Militza.

About the Stories

The Origin of Man *p.17*

This little story and the one that follows are taken from the book *Sixty Folk-Tales from Exclusively Slavonic Sources* by A.H. Wratislaw (London: Elliot Stock, 1889). They are Serbian stories from Carniola, a region in the northwest of Yugoslavia, formerly a duchy of Austria. These stories show a distinctive mingling of Christian ideas with the mythology of the pagan Slavs. Here the creation of man from drops of God's sweat (recalling beliefs such as that of the Indians of the American Southwest, who say that man was made from rubbings of the creator's skin) brings to mind the Biblical injunction, "In the sweat of thy face shalt thou eat bread, till thou return into the ground."

God's Cockerel *p.18*

This second Serbian story from Carniola is a mixture of the fall from paradise and the flood, and it leads into a very interesting cycle of stories about a godlike trickster figure called Kurent. The name of the watchman who escapes the flood is Kranyatz, and he is saved by hanging on to the vine which Kurent uses as a stick, "nourishing himself by its grapes and wine" for the nine years it takes the flood to recede. After that, Kurent and man contend for the rule of the earth, and after many struggles Kurent gains victory, by the gift of wine with which he makes man his servant.

Why Does a Cat Sit on the Doorstep in the Sun? *p.22*

This little fable is adapted from Moses Gaster's *Rumanian Bird and Beast Stories* (London: published for the Folk-Lore Society by Sidgwick & Jackson Ltd., 1916). Many folk legends are told about Noah and the ark. Sometimes Noah invites the devil on board with the ass, who is slow to embark. Noah is also said to have created the cat by rubbing the lion's nose, so that it gave birth to a cat who kept the rats on the ark under control; in a variation the lion sneezes forth a cat to chase the devil, who has entered the ark as a mouse. Sometimes the devil manages to gnaw a hole in the ark, and this is plugged either by Noah's wife with her elbow, which explains why women's elbows are always cold; or by Noah sitting on it, which explains why men always stand with their backs to the fire; or by a dog's nose, which explains why a dog's nose is always cold and wet. In medieval English mystery plays or religious pageants, Noah is shown fighting with the devil on the ark, and beating him. An account very similar to the Biblical flood story is found in the ancient Babylonian epic of Gilgamesh, dating from 3000 B.C., and the tradition of a great flood is worldwide. Stories of a primeval deluge that destroyed the first world are very common in the native mythologies of North and South America; Welsh legend celebrates Newydd Nav Neivion; the Armenians have Xisuthros, and the Serbs, Kranyatz.

The Twelve Months *p.24*

"The Twelve Months" is a Slovak story, and my version is based on the one retold by the novelist Božena Němcová in Josef Baudiš, *Czech Folk Tales* (London: George Allen & Unwin Ltd, 1917). It is an intriguing variant of the tale type known to folklorists as "The Kind and Unkind Girls." There is a study of this type of story by W.E. Roberts.

Intelligence and Luck *p.34*

This is a Czech tale from Wratislaw, *Sixty Folk-Tales from Exclusively Slavonic Sources*. This story seems to be most popular in Romania, Hungary, and Czechoslovakia.

The Wishes *p.38*

This story comes from *The Folk-Tales of the Magyars* translated and edited by The Rev. W. Henry Jones and Lewis L. Kropf (London: published for the Folk-Lore Society, 1886); it was taken from the first great collection of Hungarian *Folk-Songs and Popular Tales* collected by Janos Erdélyi. The opening paragraph is only one of many richly entertaining rigmaroles with which the Hungarians open and close their tales. The theme of the wise and foolish use of wishes is a frequent one in folktales; sometimes, as in the Grimms' "The Poor Man and the Rich Man," it is God who grants the wishes, which the poor man uses well and the rich one foolishly.

The Flying Ship *p.43*

This story was collected by the great Russian folklorist Aleksandr

Afanas'ev, and I have based my version on that in C. Fillingham Coxwell, *Siberian and Other Folk-Tales* (London: The C.W. Daniel Company, 1925). Collected from the Little Russians of the Ukraine, it is a variant of the tale type known to folklorists as "The Helpers," familiar from the Grimms' "How Six Men Got On in the World." The magic ship which sails on land and water is a common ingredient of the story, which is very popular in Eastern Europe, with many versions in Hungary, Czechoslovakia, Yugoslavia, Russia, and elsewhere. At least sixteen versions have been recorded in the Ukraine.

The Feather of Bright Finist the Falcon *p.51*

I have taken this Russian tale, which was written down in the district of Vologda, from Jeremiah Curtin's *Myths and Folk-Tales of the Russians, Western Slavs, and Magyars* (Boston: Little, Brown, and Company, 1890). It is a variant of the story known to folklorists as "The Search for the Lost Husband," which has been studied by J.Ö. Swahn in *The Tale of Cupid and Psyche*. Afanas'ev himself collected eight Russian versions of this tale, in which the prince visits the princess in the form of a bird, and is wounded by a sharp object left maliciously on the window ledge, including a story called "The Feather of Finist, the Bright Falcon," which can be found in Afanas'ev's *Russian Fairy Tales*, translated by Norbert Guterman (New York: Pantheon Books, Inc., 1945); it has a different ending to Curtin's story, but is otherwise very similar. A third version is translated as "Fenist the Bright-Eyed Falcon" in James Riordan, *Tales from Central Russia* (Harmondsworth; Kestrel Books, 1976). The strange supernatural creature known as Baba Yaga (there is either one of her or, as here, three sisters), living crammed inside her little hut which spins around on hen's legs, or riding through the air in a mortar or an iron kettle, is one of the most distinctive and memorable characters of Russian folklore.

A Clever Lass *p.61*

This Czech story, collected by Josef Kubín, is taken from Baudiš, *Czech Folk Tales*. It is a version of the story known as "The Clever Peasant Girl," of which twelve Czech versions have been recorded. It is widely told throughout Europe, and the version in Grimm is very similar to this one.

Vassilissa Golden Tress, Bareheaded Beauty *p.66*

This is taken from Curtin, *Myths and Folk-Tales of the Russians, Western*

Slavs, and Magyars, and was collected by Bronnitski. Curtin notes that the name of Tsar Svaitozar means "light-shining" or "resplendent."

How the Foolish Brother Was Drowned *p.78*

This story comes from Coxwell, *Siberian and Other Folk-Tales*. It was collected in Latvia. Latvia, Estonia, and Lithuania comprise the Baltic states of the Soviet Union, and their languages and cultures are more closely affiliated with Northern Europe than Eastern Europe, but there has inevitably been a good deal of cross-fertilization. This particular tale is probably best known in the literary retelling by Hans Christian Andersen, "Big Claus and Little Claus," but as one part of a longer tale type known as "The Rich and the Poor Peasant" it is part of the common stock of international storytelling, with many versions recorded in both Eastern and Northern Europe. Often a parson is tricked into entering the sack on the promise that he will be taken in it to heaven.

Cinder Jack *p.80*

This story was collected by Erdélyi and is taken from Jones and Kropf's *Folk-Tales of the Magyars*. It bears some relation to the male versions of the Cinderella story, in which a magic ox carries the boy through woods of copper, silver, and gold where the boy picks twigs with magic powers, but I do not know any other story quite like it. The opening in which the three sons are set to guard the vineyard is fairly common; in "The Lame Fox," a lovely Serbian version of the story known to us as the Grimms' "Golden Bird," the sons each ask their father, "Why does your right eye always laugh and your left eye always weep?" The answer is that his vineyard is being robbed each night, and again it is the simpleton brother who, with the help of a fox, puts all to rights.

Goldenhair *p.84*

This Czech story is taken from Wratislaw's *Sixty Folk-Tales from Exclusively Slavonic Sources*. The basic story is well known from the Grimms' "The White Snake," but there are various distinctively Slavic elements to this telling, in particular the two kinds of water, of death and of life.

Cinder-Stick *p.94*

This version of the familiar "Brave Tailor" story comes from Georgia and

155

is taken from Lucy Menzies, *Caucasian Folk-Tales*. A Div is a type of giant or ogre.

The Useless Wagoner *p.99*

This story was collected by László Merényi, and translated by Jeremiah Curtin in his *Myths and Folk-Tales of the Russians, Western Slavs, and Magyars*. It is a version of the internationally told folk comedy known as "The Rabbit-herd."

The Longed-for Hedgehog *p.107*

This very brief account of the tale best known as the Grimms' "Hans My Hedgehog" is a Polish story from Coxwell, *Siberian and Other Folk-Tales*.

The Golden Apples and the Nine Peahens *p.109*

This Bulgarian story was collected by Konstantin Pavlof, and translated in Wratislaw, *Sixty Folk-Tales from Exclusively Slavonic Sources*. It offers a veritable feast of folktale incidents and ingredients; the final part of the tale echoes the well-known Russian story of "Maria Morevna," in which the serpent-like creature who is called a "dragon" here is identified as Koschey the Deathless, the "Immortal Bony" of "Prince Unexpected."

A Good Deed Is Always Requited with Ill *p.122*

This Lithuanian story is also from Coxwell's *Siberian and Other Folk-Tales*. The bitter moral of this cynical little story was no doubt applicable to many of the experiences of the peasants who told and listened to it, though it is, of course, a joke rather than a serious commentary on life. There is a very similar story in Afanas'ev's *Russian Fairy Tales*, "Old Favors Are Soon Forgotten."

Prince Unexpected *p.125*

This is a Polish story taken from Wratislaw, *Sixty Folk-Tales from Exclusively Slavonic Sources*. "Immortal Bony" is the same ruler of the underworld who appears in such Russian stories as "Koschey the Deathless" and "Maria Morevna" in Afanas'ev's *Russian Fairy Tales*. The name Koschey derives from the Russian word *kost* meaning bone, hence Wratislaw's translation "Bony" and James Riordan's "Old Bones." The basic story of this folktale is one of the most popular in the European tradition, and is known as "The Girl as Helper in the Hero's Flight." Afanas'ev collected a number of stories, for instance "The Water King and Vassilissa the Wise," which are closely related to "Prince Unexpected."

The Cottage in the Sky *p.137.*

This White Russian story from Byelorussia is taken from Coxwell, *Siberian and Other Folk-Tales*. It is in essence the same story as "Jack and the Beanstalk," though the giant is replaced by the goats with two, three and four sets of eyes and ears. These were perhaps imported into this tale of a wish-fulfillment upper world via a version of the Cinderella-variant "One Eye, Two Eyes and Three Eyes." To a hungry peasant, the idea of a cottage in the sky made entirely of good food would have been very attractive, and it is found in a number of similar tales; Afanas'ev collected one in which the grandfather who climbs the beanstalk finds a cottage with "walls of pancakes, benches of white bread, and a stove of buttered curds," inhabited by twelve sister-goats. He manages to deceive them all except the one with twelve eyes, which captures him.

The Wizard *p.142*

This brief legend about a weather-working wizard was collected by P. Kulish in the Ukraine. I have adapted it from Wratislaw's *Sixty Folk-Tales from Exclusively Slavonic Sources*.

Fate *p.144*

This Serbian tale was collected by Vuk Karadžić and translated by Wratislaw in his *Sixty Folk-Tales from Exclusively Slavonic Sources*. This type of story is known to folklorists as "The Journey in Search of Fortune"; the questions posed along the way, and Fate's answers, link this story with tales such as the Grimms' "The Devil with the Three Golden Hairs."